5

Praise for the Kenni Lowry Mystery Series

"Fabulous fun and fantastic fried food! Kappes nails small town mystery with another must-read hit. (Also, I want to live in Cottonwood, KY.) Don't miss this one!"

– Darynda Jones,
New York Times Bestselling Author of *Eighth Grave After Dark*

"Packed with clever plot twists, entertaining characters, and plenty of red herrings! *Fixin' To Die* is a rollicking, delightful, down-home mystery."

– Ann Charles,
USA Today Bestselling Author of the Deadwood Mystery Series

"Southern and side-splitting funny! *Fixin' To Die* has captivating characters, nosy neighbors, and is served up with a ghost and a side of murder."

– Duffy Brown,
Author of the Consignment Shop Mysteries

"This story offers up a small touch of paranormal activity that makes for a fun read...A definite "5-star," this is a great mystery that doesn't give up the culprit until the last few pages."

– *Suspense Magazine*

"A Southern-fried mystery with a twist that'll leave you positively breathless."

– Susan M. Boyer,
USA Today Bestsel̶l̶i̶ ̶ ̶ ̶ ̶ ̶ ̶ ̶ ̶ ̶ ̶ ̶ ̶ ̶ ̶ ̶ ̶ *ook Club*

D1248808

"A wonderful series filled with adventure, a ghost, and of course some romance. This is a hard book to put down."
— *Cozy Mystery Book Reviews*

"Kappes captures the charm and quirky characters of small-town Kentucky in her new mystery...a charming, funny story with exaggerated characters. The dialect-filled quirky sayings and comments bring those characters to life."
— *Lesa's Book Critiques*

"With a fantastic cast of characters and a story filled with humor and murder you won't be able to put it down."
— *Shelley's Book Case*

"Funny and lively...Before you blink you're three chapters down and you're trying to peek ahead to see what happens next. Fast moving with great characters that you wish were real so that you might be able to visit with them more often."
— *The Reading Room*

"Kappes is an incredible author who weaves fabulous stories...I can't wait to see what she comes up next in this series."
— *Community Bookstop*

"I am totally hooked. The people of Cottonwood feel like dear friends, and I enjoy reading about the latest happenings...The story is well-told, with plenty of action and suspense, along with just enough humor to take the edge off."
— *Book Babble*

DEAD AS A
DOORNAIL

**The Kenni Lowry Mystery Series
by Tonya Kappes**

A KENNI LOWRY MYSTERY

DEAD AS A DOORNAIL

TONYA KAPPES

HENERY PRESS

Copyright

DEAD AS A DOORNAIL
A Kenni Lowry Mystery
Part of the Henery Press Mystery Collection

First Edition | May 2018

Henery Press, LLC
www.henerypress.com

All rights reserved. No part of this book may be used or reproduced in any manner whatsoever, including internet usage, without written permission from Henery Press, LLC, except in the case of brief quotations embodied in critical articles and reviews.

Copyright © 2018 by Tonya Kappes

This is a work of fiction. Any references to historical events, real people, or real locales are used fictitiously. Other names, characters, places, and incidents are the product of the author's imagination, and any resemblance to actual events or locales or persons, living or dead, is entirely coincidental.

Trade Paperback ISBN-13: 978-1-63511-334-1
Digital epub ISBN-13: 978-1-63511-335-8
Kindle ISBN-13: 978-1-63511-336-5
Hardcover ISBN-13: 978-1-63511-337-2

Printed in the United States of America

To the Kappes Cozy Krew

Chapter One

"Hey, Tina," Lucy Ellen Lowell greeted Tina Bowers, owner of Tiny Tina's Salon and Spa, as she shimmied her robust chest in front of the pedicure chair where I was sitting.

Tina was crouched down by my feet, slathering some sort of gritty lotion on my shins. "Hey, Kenni," Lucy Ellen said in a breathy tone.

Lucy's beady green eyes focused on Tina from underneath the wide-brimmed hat on top of her head. Tina's brown eyes were flat as she looked up at me from underneath her brows, not looking at Lucy Ellen at all. Slowly, Tina's jaw moved from side to side with each chew of her gum.

"Tina, you have to do my nails. I have to have them done for the upcoming wedding." Lucy Ellen paused. "I called to make an appointment, but Cheree told me that you weren't taking appointments and I have to get my nails done before Saturday and today is the only day I got open." Lucy Ellen gave Cheree Rath, Tina's employee, an ungrateful raised brow and scowl before she flung her fingers in the air. She was right. Her nails were chipped and in desperate need of painting. "Look here. These are awful. You ain't working, Kenni?" Lucy Ellen continued to show spirit hands, nail side out to Tina.

"I'm actually having a day off." I forced a smile.

It was difficult to take a day off since I was sheriff of our small town of Cottonwood, Kentucky.

"Betty and Finn are holding down the fort," I assured her when I saw from her contorted face that her brain was flipping through names like a Rolodex for who was at the sheriff's department. Betty Murphy was the department dispatch operator and secretary. Finn Vincent was the only sheriff's deputy in the department outside of my four-legged deputy, Duke, my hound dog.

"Finn gave Kenni the gift card. They're an item now." Tina winked. "That's why she's getting extra special love." She kneaded and massaged my calves with her thumbs.

"Sweet." Lucy's face pinched. "Now." Her hands plunged in front of Tina's face. "What about my nails?"

The bell over the salon door dinged.

Everyone in the salon stopped when Polly Parker and four of her friends, along with her mother, nearly fell over themselves as they pushed through the door, giggling.

"We'll be right with you." Cheree said over her shoulder with her fingers stuck in a customer's shampooed hair in the black rinsing sink.

Polly's friends were no doubt here for her wedding that was only five days away, if you included today.

"Go on and pick out some colors if you want color," Tina followed up, ignoring Lucy. "They're here for what's called a preview party."

I smiled and nodded, feeling a wee bit sorry for Tina. Polly was high maintenance even outside of being a bride. I'd imagined she was a bridezilla. Her wedding to Mayor Ryland was the talk of the town. All the small boutiques in town were selling out of dresses and knick-knacks the happy couple registered for. It was actually an event I was looking forward to as well.

"Well?" Lucy Ellen pulled the towel off of the arm of my pedicure chair and wiped the dripping sweat from her brow. I looked between her and Tina.

"Well?" Lucy Ellen asked again and cocked her leg to the side, her curvy bottom following, almost smacking into Jolee Fischer, my best friend, who was sitting in the pedicure chair next to me.

Tina's hands felt like a Brillo Pad as she rapidly rubbed them up and down my legs.

Lucy Ellen pulled her diamond-encrusted gold watch up to her round face and checked out the time. "I've got time now. And..." Her mouth formed an "O" as if she'd just remembered something very important. "Dr. Shively said you could do my toes, but don't put them in the tub since I've been nursing that big bunion and all."

"Lucy, I don't have time today." Tina chomped her gum like a cow chewing the cud as she splashed water on my shins to get the gritty stuff off, not giving even a looksie toward Lucy Ellen.

Cheree put her client under one of those big umbrella hair dryers and plopped herself down in front of Jolee to finish up.

"We are booked solid." Tina took my feet out of the water and patted them dry before picking up a bottle of natural-colored nail polish that I'd picked out, giving the bottle a couple of good whacks against the palm of her hand.

"What do you mean, Tina? I even brought my own flip flops." Lucy Ellen let an exhausted sigh and patted her purse that was slung over her shoulder. "I've been coming here for two years," she cried out. "Today is the only day I've got open before the wedding." Lucy Ellen looked over at Polly. Her eyes squinted and she nodded her head once the fake smile was across her lips. "You've always taken me when I come in."

Lucy Ellen wasn't letting up. She jerked the floppy hat off her head. Her black hair sprang out like coils. Tina choked back a laugh. I kept my eyes on her and didn't dare look at Lucy.

"And my hair needs a treatment awfully bad. And only you can do it, Tina. Only you." Lucy Ellen made a desperate attempt to jam the hair back under the hat, but the hair wasn't having it. With another failed attempt, the hair won and Lucy Ellen shoved the hat underneath her armpit.

"I'm the only one in town," Tina muttered under her breath while she started painting my toes. "That's why I'm her only one." Tina made a good point.

"You can do my hair treatment and let it sit while you paint my toes and then shampoo the treatment out. My hair can air dry while you give me a manicure." Lucy Ellen had it all figured out. "I've got cash."

She reached in her purse and pulled out a fistful of cash.

"Today isn't good. After Kenni and Jolee, we're have Polly's entire wedding party in for a preview look." Tina made it very clear she didn't have time for Lucy Ellen.

Any time I'd ask her about the rocks, she'd swear up one end and down the next that she'd bought the rocks from a beauty supply shop. It was a known fact that Tina Bowers hadn't bought the rocks because I'd received several phone calls from dispatch that Tina was down at the Kentucky River taking rocks off the side of the road when in fact it was against the law to pillage the limestone. Sure as shinola, the rocks under my piggies at the moment were jagged pieces of limestone.

"Preview look?" Lucy's head jerked toward the front of the salon and stared at Polly. "What on earth is that?" Her nose curled. She didn't give Polly a second to respond until she said, "I'm looking forward to seeing the mayor. I've not seen him in months."

"Mmhm." Polly Parker's chin lifted up and down with pride. Her lips parted into a smile that showed off her bright white veneers—a smile that reminded me of a horse's mouth. "Tina is going to paint all my bridesmaids' nails to make sure the color will match their dresses." Polly's shoulders lifted to her ears as her sweet Southern voice escalated. "Each dress is a different color. *Gone with the Wind* style." She lifted the back of her hand to her forehead as if she were going to faint. "I didn't want any surprises when we come back for the real manicures and pedicures."

Jolee and I looked at each other when Polly said *Gone with the Wind* and bit back our laughter.

"I've never heard of such a thing." Lucy Ellen tsked. "This is taking too much of Tina's time. Cheree, can't you take Tina's clients? I've got to get my hair and nails done." Lucy Ellen stormed over to Cheree, who was finishing up painting Jolee's toenails.

"I'm sorry, Lucy. We are booked to the gills and we just can't fit you in." Cheree pushed back a stray strand of her long red hair that had found a way out of her low ponytail. Her freckles deepened as the anger swelled up in her. She made it perfectly clear to Lucy, but Lucy Ellen just wasn't having it.

"You can squeeze me into a wee little spot." Lucy Ellen continued to look around the shop. "I've been coming here for two years." She held up two fingers in the air and flip-flopped them around saying it for a second time as if they didn't hear her the first or they didn't realize she'd been coming that long.

"And in those two years," Cheree sounded as if she'd had enough, "you've cancelled at least a dozen times." She looked up over the rim of her glasses from the stool in front of Jolee and stared at Lucy. She had a bottle of open polish in one hand and the nail brush in the other. "Did you ever think of the financial bind you put us in when you don't show up? How are we gonna pay our bills? Did you ever think of that?"

"Then I'll buy the Perfectly Posh." Lucy Ellen picked up the bottle from Tina's nail station and looked at it. "This isn't Perfectly Posh. Where is it?"

She gripped a much lighter pink version in her hand that clearly didn't match her chipped up fingernails.

"You know I don't sell my polish to no one." Tina sprayed down the foot tub and gave it a couple of scrubs to clean it out.

She stood up, tugged the scrunchie from her wrist, and pulled her brown hair in a top knot on her head. She stretched her neck into a slow roll and strolled over to Lucy Ellen like she was gearing up for a confrontation.

"If you ain't gonna do my nails for Polly's wedding, then I'll have someone else do them with your polish," Lucy Ellen said through gritted teeth with another polish in her grips. "You are the only person who knows how to make your own polish that no one else has and I can't have the same polish as the other girls from the Hunt Club at the wedding. I just can't," she cried, clutching the polish to her chest.

Tina plucked the bottle of homemade nail polish right out of Lucy's hand.

"I don't even have any Perfectly Posh made up. Get out of here." Tina's tone meant business. Lucy Ellen slid her eyes past Tina's shoulders and looked at me. I offered a pinched smile.

It was probably time for me to step in even though I wasn't on duty. I went to stand up, but Jolee caught my attention. She shook her head for me to stay out of it.

She whispered, "This is the best part about coming to the beauty shop." Jolee laughed. "All the crazy comes out of people."

The tension crept up my back and into my shoulders. *Wasn't this supposed to be a relaxing experience?* I thought and continued to look down.

"Well, I never. You'll regret this, Tina Bowers." Lucy Ellen twirled her finger around the shop. "Tiny Tina's will no longer be in business once it gets out in all the gossip circles how you treated me here today." Lucy Ellen brought her hands up to her chest. "I'm sending in a bad review to the *Chronicle* as soon as I get home."

"Lucy," Cheree called after her before she left, "you might oughta try a wet comb on that cowlick of yours."

Lucy Ellen huffed and puffed before she turned on the balls of her feet and trotted out the door. Bouncy hair and all.

"Good riddance." Tina snapped her fingers and pointed for me to move over to the nail station for my manicure. "She's always sending bad reviews to the *Chronicle*."

I walked on the heels of my feet, careful not to smear the fresh polish on my toes.

"Geez, I can't believe the gall of that woman." Tina jerked my hand over the puffy brown pillow and adjusted the miniature light over my hand. "Scoot up," she instructed me.

"If she had another wrinkle on that body, she'd be able to screw on that hat," Cheree said under her breath as she finished up painting Jolee's toenails and moved her to a manicure station next to me, sticking Jolee's fingers in a bowl of water for her cuticles to soften.

She walked over to the client under the dryer and felt around her head before she started the dryer back up.

"Lucy's an awful woman. She had the nerve to order from my food truck and bring the food back half eaten with a fly in it saying I cooked the fly in the food when I know good and well the fly flew into her food after she sat down at the picnic table because she'd spent the first few minutes batting them away." Jolee curled her nose. "While stuffing her face the whole time."

Cheree busied herself cleaning out the foot tub where Jolee had been and filled it right back up, motioning for Polly to come on over.

"My mama made me invite her to the wedding. I didn't want to." Polly gave her mom a sideways look. "I didn't want to invite any of them hunting club women, but Mama insisted since I'm gonna be the first lady and all. Plus, Chance is a member of the club. Not that he goes all that much, but it's good for his position as mayor."

Polly fanned her face with her fingers.

"I sure hope the weather is good next weekend." Polly looked over at her mother.

Paula Parker didn't pay her daughter any attention. She just continued to sit in the plastic chair in the front of the shop flipping through the five-year-old beauty magazines.

"You obviously invited them." Cheree turned the cold water on a little more after Polly sat down and stuck her big toe in and pulled it right back out.

"I told Tibbie Bell to go ahead and invite them all." Polly referred to another friend of mine who was the only wedding planner in Cottonwood. "Chance told me not to worry my pretty little head because this week is their annual gun show, which means the men have taken off work the next couple of weeks to get their cabins ready for the first week of hunting season." Polly sucked in a deep breath and slowly let it out with a humming sound.

"Tibbie told me to breathe when I felt myself getting a little anxious over the wedding. Them women sure do make me anxious." She took another deep breath.

"Now, now." Paula Parker hurried over to Polly and drew her into her arms. "Don't be going and getting yourself all worked up." They hugged for an uncomfortable few seconds.

With a pouty mouth, Polly picked up a bottle of nail polish and looked at the bottom before she set it down and picked up another one. She did the same thing bottle after bottle. All the women in the salon waited to hear what Polly was talking about. It was just how it worked around our small town. Gossip not only bound us together but also tore us apart.

"Lucy Ellen called me about the food." Jolee laughed and threw in her two cents worth of gossip.

"She did what?" Paula Parker's voice escalated. "The nerve," she gasped. "I'm paying you too much money if you ask me," Paula muttered under her breath but loud enough for me to hear.

"Yeah. She wanted to know what we were serving to the guests so she could plan out if she needed to eat before the wedding in case she didn't like the food." Jolee shook her head.

"Maybe you should slip a mickey in her cocktail at the beginning of the wedding so she'll be knocked out." Polly shrugged, half-joking, half-serious.

"Maybe I should slip her more than a mickey," Jolee agreed. "She thinks she can go around and say what she wants with no consequences. She called the fire inspector on me one week, then the health inspector the next. Then she did that article in the newspaper giving my food truck a bad review." Jolee huffed.

I'd thought she'd gotten over that incident, but apparently not.

"To this day, the Hunt Club won't let me park in front of their meetings because of that woman. She's hurting my livelihood." Jolee's foot was shaking up and down. A sure sign she was fired up. "I wish someone would put her in her place."

"I for one am very excited you're catering the wedding." Polly's chin lifted in the air, and in a swift motion, she brought it down to her right shoulder. "Right, Mama?"

"Yes, dear. Anything that comes out of your precious mouth is gold." Paula Parker smiled with pride.

"Kenni," Betty Murphy called over the walkie-talkie that I had in my purse. "Sheriff, are you there?"

I held up a wet fingernail to Tina to hold on and grabbed my purse to take out the walkie-talkie. I still kept my radio on me in case there was a dire emergency.

"I'm here, Betty," I said after I hit the button on the side.

"I hate to bother you on your day off, but we got a complaint from Lucy Ellen Lowell." Everyone's head in the entire salon shot up in the air and looked my way. "She says that she was discriminated against and wants to file a complaint. I told her that Officer Vincent was out on a call and that I'd have him call her back, but she insisted I get in touch with him immediately or she was coming down here and I just don't want to deal with Lucy Ellen Lowell this afternoon."

"Did she tell you that I was at the salon when she came in?" I asked Betty.

"I knew something was up when I told her it was your day off and she muttered something about how she and Darnell had hosted your election fundraiser. I just let that drop. So what do you want me to do?" Betty asked.

"You tell her that you talked to me and that I'll give her a call back." I clicked off and stuck the walkie-talkie back into my purse.

"Maybe I should give her a hair treatment and let the scissors slip." Tina dragged her finger across her neck.

Chapter Two

"Duke," I called from the kitchen when I got home from my so-called spa day at Tiny Tina's. "Duke."

I threw my keys on the kitchen counter and shut the kitchen door. I stood there for a second and let the quiet envelop me until I heard a loud thud, followed by the sound of the pounding of the four large paws of my trusty deputy hound dog.

All the yammering going on down at Tiny Tina's wore me out. I didn't understand how people gossiped day in and day out. All those stories started running together until I'd finally turned it off in my head.

"Hey, you big lug." I bent down and was greeted with the best slobbery kisses. "You ready to go outside?"

He danced toward the kitchen door. I opened it and walked out with him. The fresh air might help clear my head. It was that strange time in between seasons in Kentucky when the weather was hot and humid one day and cold and chilly the next. This afternoon was turning out to be more on the light breezy side that was not quite sweatshirt weather, but not tank top weather either.

"Hey. I saw your Jeep in the driveway." Finn Vincent peered over the gate that led into my backyard.

He let himself in. Before he could say anything else, I pulled him to me with a fistful of his brown deputy sheriff's shirt and laid a big kiss on him.

"You must've missed me." His eyes twinkled, sending my heart all aflutter.

"You must've been waiting by your window waiting for me to pull in," I teased. He lived a couple of houses down from me.

Though he was from the north and not a real southerner, his handsome charm hadn't gone unnoticed by every single girl in Cottonwood when he first came to town. Over the past year, he'd really picked up on the fact that in the south, it's much easier to catch flies with honey instead of vinegar and holding the door open for a woman can go a long way.

"I'm just so glad that you don't like all the girly things, because I just don't know if I could go to Tiny Tina's on a regular basis for nails, hair, and spa days. They curl way more than hair there." I rubbed my head. "My head hurts from all the gossip."

Duke darted from the far corner of the backyard when he saw his ball-throwing buddy. He was always happy to see Finn.

I sat down in a chair on my back porch and enjoyed watching Finn throw the ball to Duke a few times until Duke decided he was going to sniff all the grass along the back side of the fence.

"That bad?" He turned around and looked at me with dipped eyes. "I thought you'd like the gift card."

"I'm very appreciative of the gift card, and it came at a great time since we have the wedding next weekend and I did need my nails done, but I'm amazed at how they can just go from one gossip story to another." Goosebumps prickled my leg as he scooted his chair closer to mine.

"I get enough of their tales at Euchre. These girls do it day in and day out." I left out the part of Lucy Ellen's crazy tirade and how she'd called dispatch since I'd taken care of it. Plus, he'd probably be upset that Betty Murphy had called me on my first day off in months. "How was your day?"

"Made the usual rounds, and I got a call from Bosco Frederick from the Hunt Club. He said something about having a deputy at their annual gun show in a couple of days at The Moose Lodge." There was an amused look on his face.

These were the times that his northern roots stuck out. He didn't understand that guns and knives strapped on the belts of Cottonwood citizens were accessories that completed the look of the locals. If you weren't packing, then we knew you were an out-of-towner.

"The annual gun show." I let out a deep sigh and extended my legs out in front of me. "Polly mentioned that today. I can't believe we're only a couple weeks off from the opening of hunting season." I crossed my forearms across my belly and let the cool breeze float around me. "The Hunt Club wives host this annual show. The men all take the next couple of weeks off to clean and fix up their hunting cabins and deer stands so when the season opens, they're ready to go."

"Annual? How many more guns can people in this town own?" he joked.

"You can never have enough." I winked. "Lucy Ellen and all the women in the Hunt Club are sitting together at the wedding since their husbands are occupied."

"I just don't get all that hunting business. Poor animals." Finn had such a tender heart when it came to animals. He'd even taken in Cosmo, an orange tabby cat that belonged to one of the criminals we'd put behind bars.

"It's just a way of life around here. Plus Lucy's husband is the only person who does taxidermy here in Cottonwood, so she's got to promote her lifestyle." She could've done it a little less conspicuously, but she was harmless and had given Tina and the girls a lot to talk about and entertain me while I'd endured the Kentucky River limestones under my feet.

Duke darted along the fence line up to the gate on the side of the house and followed up with a little bit of barking, then the wagging tail, telling me whoever was walking up the sidewalk on the side of my house was someone he knew.

"There's my grand-doggie." Mama's voice carried into the backyard and made Duke's tail wag faster.

I stood up and walked over, grabbing Duke by the collar.

"Hey, Mama." I stood up. My eyes slid over Mama's shoulder.

She wasn't alone. Polly and Paula Parker were with her. Polly had a hanger in her hand and the white dress bag flowed down with the bottom edges ending in her mama's hand.

"Kenni, can you please chain up that mutt?" Polly's perfect pink-lined lips snarled. "I can't have him ruining this dress." She didn't take her eyes off Duke. He was dancing around in anticipation of the ladies coming in the yard.

I let go of his collar and snapped my fingers for him to lay down. He was a trained dog. Not that he was an official police dog, but I'd had him since he was given to me from my poppa, which was a whole 'nother story all together.

"Polly, he won't hurt you. He's a sweetie." Mama did love Duke.

When I looked at Mama, I saw exactly what I was going to look like later in life. She had shoulder-length brown hair like me. We had the same olive skin tone and if it weren't for a few wrinkles, she'd look my age. Both of us stood five feet, five inches and pretty much had the same body type, though her hips were a little bigger than mine. Only because she'd birthed me, her only child. Trust me when I say that I completely get the only child syndrome.

"Hi, Finn," Polly greeted him, as did Mrs. Parker.

"It's so good to see you in regular clothes." Mama smiled so big, bringing her shoulders up to her ears as she reached out and grabbed my hand to get a gander at the manicure. "I heard you used your gift card from Finn." Mama couldn't stop the big smile when she looked at him.

It wasn't a big secret that Mama had plans for my life other than being the sheriff. She'd planned on the biggest election of my life being voted Debutante of Cottonwood instead of being voted Sheriff.

"You are going to be such a beautiful maid of honor." She let out the biggest happiest sigh that I'd not heard since I let her take me prom-dress shopping back in high school.

"Maid of honor?" My oh-shit meter went off real fast. I started to shake my head as fast as Duke's tail had wagged when I could see what was happening. "I'm sorry," I said. "I thought I heard you say maid of honor."

"Oh, Kendrick Lowry." Polly Parker's chin-length perfectly blonde (though it came from one of Tiny Tina's bottles) hair didn't move as she bounced past Mama. She dragged that dress bag over to me. "I couldn't think of anyone else in my time of need. After all, your job description on the Cottonwood Sheriff's Department website says that the sheriff helps anyone who needs it."

Polly jerked around and handed the hanger off to Mama as she started to unzip the big dress bag.

"My time of need is right now and it's for a beer," I said to Finn and looked back at him. His hand was over his mouth and his eyes were big.

He threw his hands up in the air and stood up.

"I think it's time for me to go." His lips tremored as he tried to not smile. "I'll go grab us some supper from Kim's Buffet and give you a little girl time."

"Girl time!" Mama squealed.

"No!" I gasped and grabbed his hand. "You can't leave me. What kind of boyfriend are you?"

"One that wants to stay your boyfriend. You're gonna need some food." He bent down and kissed my cheek.

"Ta-da!" Polly screamed and pulled the hanger in the air, letting the bag fall on the ground.

"I'm out." Finn pointed his finger toward the gate and walked away, leaving me there with my mouth gaped open.

"I knew you were going to love it." Polly looked between me and the dress, her big horse teeth sparkling. Her head bobbled in delight as she looked at the hunter-green dress that looked like it'd come right off the curtain rods of an old plantation home.

Dr. Bev Houston, the local dentist, should've been arrested for giving Polly Parker those big veneers in that tiny mouth of hers.

"And we can't forget your bonnet." As if they'd rehearsed it, Paula produced a matching green bonnet. If they thought that was going on top of my head, they had another thing coming to them.

"My bonnet?" I took a few steps backward and wagged my finger in front of me.

"Of course, we'd have to get you back down to Tiny Tina's to change out the polish you picked because we are doing Perfectly Posh." Polly gave me instructions like I had no decision in this matter.

"I got Natural Nail." I wiggled my fingers as if this was the worst issue going on here. I was already plum tuckered out and they'd only been here a few minutes. My hands were shaking. I was in a pickle and it wasn't good. Polly Parker and I weren't even friends. "Tina said Natural Nail goes with everything."

"You're right." Polly's eyes squinted as she looked lovingly at my mother as if I were a toddler holding on to my mama's leg. "She doesn't know wedding etiquette at all."

They looked between each other knowingly.

"I didn't see any sort of dress code on your wedding invitation." I brought my hand up to my head and rubbed my temples and forehead.

Jolee and I had a good laugh when the invitations to Polly's wedding came and it looked exactly like something from *Gone with the Wind*. In fact, all the food Polly had contracted Jolee to cater was deep Southern dishes. But I didn't recall a dress code.

"What is wrong with you?" Mama asked. "I think them stones Tina put in your foot bath have done something to your head."

Mama was so embarrassed by my behavior she turned all of the shades of red on one of those color wheels hanging up in the art room in Cottonwood Elementary School.

"Maid of honor." Polly shook the hanger.

"You're going to be a maid of honor now that my sorority sister from college can't make it." She turned to her mama. "Can you believe that she's not coming because she just had a baby? The nerve of saying yes and then backing out."

It was just like Polly Parker to find fault with a new precious baby. I'd bet my bottom dollar that friend had gotten a gander at this dress and bailed, leaving me in the lurch. Too bad I didn't have a good excuse like a baby.

"I'm...um...I'm..." I couldn't take my eyes off the ugly dress. "I'm not even good friends with you. And I didn't do the website. Betty Murphy did."

I clearly wasn't sure what she wrote on the website. But I would definitely be making some changes.

I snapped my fingers. "What about Toots Buford? She's your best friend and I don't think she's in your wedding party."

"Toots Buford works at Dixon's Foodtown and doesn't have enough money to rub two dimes together, much less buy this three-hundred-dollar dress." She brushed the dress side to side, letting the crinoline crunch to a dramatic halt. "Your mama has not only paid me for your dress, she's even hosting the bridal-party luncheon on Friday that as maid of honor you're supposed to give."

"Well, that ain't gonna happen." The words fell out of mouth. "I've got to work."

"Kendrick Lowry!" Mama cried out and buried her head in her hands. "You sure do know how to embarrass your mama and your family in someone else's time of need." She took her face out of her hands and looked at Polly and Paula. "I raised her better than this. It's living here on Free Row that's done it to her."

Mama's head nodded as she referred to my neighborhood. Free Row was technically Broadway Street, but most of my neighbors were on commodity cheese, food stamps, and any other free things they could get from the government. Not that it was an issue, but they also had broken-down furniture on their front porches and beat-up cars hoisted up on cinder blocks. Not Mama's ideal living arrangements for her one and only child.

Still, it was my poppa's home and he left it to me in his will. I loved it as a young child and I love it as my home now. Especially now that Finn was just a couple of doors down.

"I'm not using bad manners. I'm just saying that years from now you want to look back at your photos with fond memories of each person in your wedding." I thought my reasoning sounded good and I was proud of how I'd just plucked that logic right out of my you-know-what. "Not the memory that I accused you of killing someone a year ago."

It was true. Polly Parker was a suspect in a local murder and I was relentless in proving it. Luckily, I was wrong. I should've known better because Polly Parker would never put her manicure in danger with manual labor like murder.

I watched in horror as Polly's chest started to pop up and down, followed by a turned-down mouth, watering eyes, and a full-out crying hissy fit. And it wasn't pretty. She was not a pretty crier.

"Look what you've done," Paula spouted to me through her gritted teeth. "Just you wait until the election. I don't care if you're unopposed. I'll write someone in instead of voting for you."

That did it for me.

"Fine. I love the color." I grabbed the dress out from Polly's dainty fingers and held it up to my body. "I love the dress." I couldn't stress it enough. "Perfectly Posh," I wiggled my fingers like spirit fingers, "here I come."

Chapter Three

The moment I agreed to be Polly's maid of honor, I regretted it. Not only was the dress awful, it didn't fit me. I was a solid size eight, sometimes a ten, and it was a four. There was no way I was going to stop going to Ben's Diner for my morning dose of coffee, gravy biscuits, and bacon to fit into the dress, as Polly had suggested with a look of horror on her face when she saw me stuffed into the dress like a summer sausage.

After the wedding brigade left, I wasn't much company. Finn had come back with all of my favorite dishes from Kim's Buffet, but I was in no mood to eat. All the pushing and tugging Mama did to my body to even get me in the dress left me exhausted and mentally drained. Finn went home and I decided to go to bed. Maybe sleeping it off was what I needed.

"Sheriff! Sheriff," the urgent caller's voice jolted me wide awake when I answered the phone at four o'clock the next morning.

"Get over here right away. My wife is dead!" The desperate sound of the man woke me up, but the words "my wife is dead popped me straight out of bed."

Duke leapt off the bed. It wasn't unusual for a small-town sheriff like me to give out their phone number or be listed in the phone book. Small town, small ways.

"Who is this?" I asked, the phone stuck in between my ear and shoulder.

I hopped around on one foot while trying to shove one leg and then the other in my sheriff's pants.

"Oh my God," the man's voice cried. "Lucy!" The sobs from the man dragged out. "Lucy Ellen baby, Lucy Ellen baby. Lucy Ellen baby, wake up."

"Lucy? Sir, I'm gonna need you to calm down. Tell me where you live." The only Lucy Ellen I knew was Lucy Ellen Lowell and she looked perfectly healthy to me at Tiny Tina's yesterday.

"It's Darnell Lowell. I just got home from huntin' and she's...she's...not waking up."

"Darnell, don't move her. I'll be right there." I clicked off my phone and immediately dialed EMT services to get an ambulance over there, which was what Lowell should've done before he called me. But sometimes things were done ass-backward around these parts.

"Let's go, Duke!" I yelled down the hall.

It was too early in the morning to call Mrs. Brown, my next-door neighbor, to take care of him. I shoved some of his kibble in my pants pocket, grabbed a to-go coffee mug, ignoring the fact I was pouring what was left from yesterday morning's coffee pot, and heated it in the microwave. While the coffee warmed, I strapped on my holster around my waist and attached the walkie-talkie on my shoulder.

The last thing I grabbed as I ran out of my house was my bag with all the tools I needed for a crime scene and my Jeep Wagoneer keys. I opened the door to let Duke jump in and tugged the kibble out of my pocket, throwing it on the seat for him to gobble up since I didn't know how long I was going to be at the Lowell house. I stuck my mug in the bean-bag coffee holder that laid across the hump in the floorboard and jabbed my keys in the ignition.

In a fluid motion, I grabbed the old police siren from underneath my seat and licked the suction cup. With my free hand, I manually cranked down the driver's window and stuck the siren up on the roof, skimming the side of it with the pad of my finger to turn on the flashing red light and siren.

With the pedal to the floor and Duke hanging out the passenger window, the Wagoneer rattled down Broadway. Without stopping, I took a right at the end onto Main Street. The Lowells lived out in a subdivision off the bypass and the quickest way to get there was to drive south on Main Street until the flashing light to turn right on the bypass going toward Harrodsburg, another city near Cottonwood. It was a big deal with the input of the bypass around Cottonwood a few years back. The road was built around the outskirts of Cottonwood for unnecessary traffic through Cottonwood.

The houses were ranch style and had been built back in the seventies. Each house had a fairly good amount of property. Just enough to have neighbors, but far away enough to feel like you were in the country with a horse or two or even a nice big garden.

Darnell was pacing back and forth when I pulled up. There were a set of headlights barreling down the drive practically as soon as I got the Jeep in park. It was Finn in his Dodge Charger.

"Kenni." Darnell's face was as white as the inside of a freshly cut turnip. His thick black curly hair sat on top his head. "What am I gonna do?" His eyes searched mine as he wrung his hands. "I swear she's dead. I know how to feel for a pulse. I'm a hunter."

"Hold on. The ambulance will be here shortly." I wanted to offer him some hope. The chill in the night air put a stiffness in my bones as if it knew and was telling me something. "Where is she?"

"Right on in there." His chin fell to his chest as he shook his head. He still had on his camouflage hunting overalls with a lime-green Henley shirt. The members of the Hunt Club had a rule that they had to wear something neon so they wouldn't mistake one another for a deer or whatever it happened to be they were hunting.

Finn walked up with his uniform shirt partially buttoned and his white tee underneath.

"I heard your siren going off, so I jumped up and followed you." Finn was a great deputy. A grateful smile floated across my lips. "What's going on?"

"Darnell, why don't you wait right here while Deputy Vincent and I go in and see what's going on." I nodded and put my hand on his forearm to give him some sort of comfort.

Finn and I walked through the front door. There was a small foyer with what looked like an office to the right. The foyer led into a hallway that if you looked clear down it, you could see the refrigerator. Before you reached the kitchen, there was a step-down family room. And that's where I saw her.

"Lucy Ellen Lowell." I pointed at her feet sticking out from around the corner of the couch.

"Is she dead?" Finn asked as we hurried to her side.

I bent down. Her eyes were glazed over and her skin had already turned blue. I felt for a pulse that clearly wasn't there on her neck and then on her wrist.

"Dead as a doornail." My poppa's ghost stood in the dark corner of the room with his eyes focused on the lifeless body of Lucy Ellen Lowell.

Chapter Four

My heart pounded and my stomach churned. There was only one reason Poppa would be visiting me from the Great Beyond. That reason was murder, and the only dead person was Lucy Ellen Lowell, which, if you put two and two together, meant she was murdered.

I knew her heart wasn't going to start beating. I knew there wasn't going to be a pulse no matter how many times I checked or where I felt for it. But I couldn't say it out loud. Seeing Poppa's ghost and interacting with him was the only secret I'd kept from Finn. You see, a year or so ago, there'd been little to no crime in Cottonwood, and of course I took pride in thinking that it was because I was such a badass sheriff. Truth be told, my Poppa's ghost had been running off any would-be crime, not only keeping the crime rate low but also keeping me safe. That was good and dandy until two crimes happened at the same time in Cottonwood. Apparently even a ghost can't be in two places at once, and that's when I first saw the ghost of my poppa.

Once those crimes were solved, he'd disappeared. It wasn't until there was yet another murder in Cottonwood and then another that Poppa showed up again. Then I realized that Poppa's ghost only showed up when there'd been a murder in

Cottonwood and he was there as my deputy ghost. This was how I knew that Lucy Ellen Lowell was, in fact...murdered.

Again, I reached down with my index finger and middle finger together, acting like I was checking for a pulse. My fingers moved onto her wrist, but the pigment on her face told me she'd been there for a few hours. I tried to calculate the time of death, which I guessed was probably three hours ago, but I'd leave that bit of information for Max Bogus, the coroner, to determine.

"I told you she's a goner." Poppa ghosted himself over to me. "And you've still got this one here?" His head thrust sideways, nodding at Finn.

I bit my lip and kept a poker face, ignoring Poppa. He liked Finn as a deputy, just not as my boyfriend.

"Do you think it was a heart attack?" Finn asked. "Looks like a heart attack. I don't see any wounds or blood. It looks like she fell while doing a crossword puzzle."

I needed to stay calm and not blurt out that Lucy Ellen had been murdered because Finn couldn't see my Poppa. Only Duke and I could see Poppa. Only I could talk to him.

"We still need to process the scene just in case." I knew this was going to make Finn question me and I had to sound calm even with the exploding feeling going off inside me that we had a homicide case on our hands.

I took the toe of my shoe and slid a crossword-puzzle book out from underneath her.

"Pfft. Doing a crossword puzzle." Poppa brushed Finn off. "Someone was crossing her off of this earth. That's what went on here." Poppa stomped around, his eyes darting around the shag carpet that I was sure hadn't been replaced since it was laid.

"Will you go get my bag out of the Wagoneer and make sure Duke's okay?" I asked Finn, who readily agreed.

It'd give me a minute to talk to Sheriff Elmer Sims.

"Hi, Poppa." I smiled so big when we locked eyes. He was the reason I'd gotten into law enforcement and without him, the last few murders in Cottonwood would've taken a lot longer to solve. "I hate that something awful has happened to Lucy, but I do love seeing you."

"Kenni-bug." Hearing my nickname from his lips brought a sense of peace that made me feel like I was going to be able to get down to the nitty gritty of this crime and fast.

"Let's get to work." He vigorously rubbed his hands together.

His broad shoulders dropped from underneath his brown sheriff's uniform that we'd buried him in.

"Lucy Ellen never hurt no one. She might be a little pushy and a bit nosy, but who'd do this to her?" he asked like he used to do when I was a child and he'd be working on a case. It was the beginning of the who, why, and why not game we'd play with one another to help solve the crimes. We were a dynamic duo while he was alive, and even after.

"I don't know. But she did make a few enemies over the last few weeks." I looked down at my hands and at the Natural Nail fingernail color. I couldn't help but recall how she'd acted yesterday when she showed up at Tiny Tina's. "Tina Bowers was one of them. When Tina said she couldn't do her nails, Lucy Ellen had a near fit in the shop. Even called Betty at dispatch to make a complaint."

"That can't be." Poppa squatted down near her torso, where her hands were off to the side. "Her nails look perfect to me."

There was a gun cabinet in the corner full of shotguns and a couple of handguns. Those always got my attention.

"Perfectly Posh," I gasped. My heart sank right into my feet. "Tiny Tina's," I whispered, knowing it was the exact match of Tina Bower's homemade nail polish Lucy Ellen had tried to purchase the day before.

I also knew that Tina didn't sell her nail polish. Which begged the question: how did Lucy's nails get painted the exact same color as Tina's Perfectly Posh? My eyes shifted around the room to see if I could spot a bottle of nail polish. The snap of the closure on my utility belt echoed throughout the quiet house when I took my flashlight out and shined it around the room in the dark crevices. Nothing jumped out at me.

And it didn't help matters that I knew Tina and Lucy Ellen had gotten into it. I shuddered. The image of Tina dragging her finger across her neck was an image I wished I could forget, but her words were the most haunting part.

"Maybe I should give her a hair treatment and let the scissors slip."

"Did you hear me?" Finn broke me out of my thoughts.

"No. No. I'm sorry. I was just thinking." I reached out and took the bag. "What were you saying?"

I unzipped the bag and took out my camera and notepad. I quickly wrote down "Perfectly Posh" and snapped a couple of photos, especially of Lucy's fingernails. I couldn't be 100 percent sure, but I was darn near 95 percent sure that it was the same exact color.

"I said that the EMTs are here and I told them to come on in." His words were barely out of his mouth before they came in. "Why are you taking photos like it's a crime scene?"

"Hey guys," I greeted them. None of us looked wide awake. It had to be around five a.m. by now and dawn was barely sneaking up on the horizon. "Do you think you could be careful? I'm not sure if this is a crime scene or not. I just need confirmation that she's expired."

I'd always hated that word. Expired. Such a sad word.

"We are sure it's a crime scene." Poppa's ghost could get

very frustrated with me really fast when he felt like I wasn't listening to him.

I gave him a blank stare. He glared and huffed to the side as the EMTs started to work on Lucy.

"Who were you whispering to when I came back in?" Finn put the palm of his hand on the small of my back. It was nice and comforting.

"Myself. Like always." My standard reply when he'd find me talking to the air, even though I was actually talking to Poppa. "Let's go talk to Darnell," I suggested and headed back down the hallway. "Something doesn't seem right here," I said over my shoulder and walked out of the house.

The fog had rolled in from the Kentucky River and lay across the yard in front of their house. The burnt-orange fall morning told me the sun was peeking out and would soon lift the fog, making it another beautiful fall day in the Bluegrass state.

"Darnell, can you tell me how exactly you found Lucy Ellen?" I asked.

I put down my bag and had my pencil ready to write down what he was telling me.

"I left a couple of days ago with the boys for our annual trip to get my cabin and deer stand ready. Lucy Ellen was upset because she didn't want to go to the mayor's wedding alone. I kissed her goodbye and left. A couple of the guys had gotten some wild hogs, since it's only wild hog season until we can hunt deer. The refrigerator at our hunting cabin was on the fritz so I told them I'd drive them home and see Lucy Ellen 'cause she left a message on my cell all upset over something." His voice cracked as he recalled the last time he'd seen his wife. When he drew his hand up and through his hair, it exposed a handgun tucked in the waistband of his pants.

"Do you have a concealed carry?" I nodded to the gun. I had a rule to keep myself protected before I could protect the rest of Cottonwood.

"Yes, ma'am." He nodded and pulled out his wallet where he kept his certificate.

"What was she upset about? Did she say?" I asked, taking a good look at the paper before I gave it back to him.

"Something about not being ready for the wedding and some appointments getting mixed up with her nails. She was always getting something lifted, tucked, and redone. I could never keep up." His eyes clouded with tears. "Whatever made her happy made me happy. Me and that old gal been married for forty-five years. I was gonna retire soon and we were gonna live the life." His lips pressed together in a duck-bill look.

I offered a weak smile and wrote down what he'd said.

The EMTs came out of the house with an empty gurney and their bags zipped up. They shook their heads.

"We called Max Bogus and let him know. He should be here any minute." One of them referred to the town's coroner and owner of the only funeral home in Cottonwood.

Naturally, it was the next step in the process of removing the body even if it wasn't a crime scene. Cottonwood was so small it only took someone ten minutes to drive across town, and that's if they were driving twenty-five miles an hour and got stopped at all three traffic lights.

"I told her to get her blood pressure checked out. She'd just gone to see Camille down in town for her diabetes." Darnell's eyes were filled with tears. "Do you think she just dropped dead of a heart attack? She always said she wanted to go fast. Did she go fast?"

In the blink of an eye, there was a hearse rolling up the driveway.

It was always hard to see people grieve. In my line of duty, I saw that more than I saw happy tears.

"I'm sorry, Darnell. I can't answer those questions for you right now." I stepped out of the way as Max Bogus rolled the church cart past us and into the house.

Chapter Five

"Why did you take all that time to process the Lowell house when there wasn't anything to point to a homicide?" Finn plucked the menu from between the salt and pepper shakers after we sat down in our regular table at Ben's Diner.

"Things aren't always as they seem." Poppa sighed and licked his lips when Ben showed up with three coffees. One for Finn and two for me. Ben was good at keeping my caffeine addiction fueled. "He should know that coming from a big-city police department." Poppa scoffed.

Ben pulled a dog treat from his front pocket and gave it to Duke. Duke wagged his tail and happily took a few scratches behind the ears from Ben.

"Here you go." Ben dropped a handful of creamer cups and the *Cottonwood Chronicle* on the table. He lifted the backward hat off his shaggy head of brown hair just enough to grab the pencil he'd stuck behind his ear. "What'll ya have?"

"The usual?" He looked at me, knowing I wanted some biscuits and gravy.

"With a drizzle of chocolate added." I pulled both cups of steaming coffee to me, cupped the creamers, and dragged those over too.

Duke laid down next to my chair, pushing my feet to the

side to make room for him.

"Uh-oh." Ben's brows cocked over his brown eyes. "Bad morning already?" He looked at his bare wrist. "You never have a drizzle of chocolate this early."

"You could say my morning could've started out better." I took a drink of the much-needed cup of joe. "Darnell Lowell found Lucy Ellen deceased this morning."

"That's terrible." Ben's forehead wrinkled. "How?"

"Natural causes" came out of Finn's mouth and "We aren't sure" came out of my mouth at the same time.

"Which is it?" Ben looked between the two of us.

"We aren't sure." I picked up the cup and took a sip.

"I'll have the breakfast hot brown." Finn put the menu back and clasped his hands around his cup of coffee.

I glanced through the paper while Finn and Ben chitchatted about the local high-school football team that was making big state news for the upcoming fall season. Plus the quarterback had some D1 college scouting him over the season.

Just like every other woman in Cottonwood, I flipped to what was known as Page Two. Page Two was really page two, but it had all the social gossip that was going on in Cottonwood and I was sure something about Polly Parker's maid of honor dropping out had to be in there. Boy, was I caught off guard to see a photo of Tina Bowers standing out front of her shop with her hand planted on her hip looking as if she were fussing at someone. On the right corner of the photo was another photo that showed Tina on the side of the road picking up limestones. The headline read "Tiny Tina's Small-Town Fraud," and was written by none other than Lucy Ellen Lowell.

Ben headed back to the kitchen.

"Here is why I think it could be more than just a heart attack." I turned the paper around and pushed it across the table.

Silently I sipped my coffee and watched Finn read. It certainly was the highlight of my morning. I could watch him all day long. I smiled and brought my cup up to my lips.

"Really?" Poppa rolled his eyes. "Leave all the goo-goo-ga-ga for later. We've got to go visit Tina Bowers." He stood behind Finn and pointed to the paper.

"There are always these sorts of crazy reviews in here every week from her. A couple of weeks ago there was one in there about the Pet Patch not carrying some sort of dog food." His lip drew up, his nose curled. "Don't forget about the one she did on Jolee's food truck."

"I agree. But I witnessed an argument between Tina and Lucy Ellen yesterday that's going to be hard to forget now that Lucy Ellen is dead." I dragged my finger across my neck like Tina had done. "Tina did this and said that maybe she should do Lucy's hair and let the scissors slip."

"Why would she say that?" Finn asked. This time he took a little more interest.

"Apparently Lucy Ellen has a bad habit of not showing up or cancelling appointments. She also just strolls into Tiny Tina's when she needs something done and expects them to accommodate her right then." I took another drink of my coffee. I continued, "Yesterday Tina had booked all of Polly Parker's pre-wedding appointments and Lucy Ellen was so mad because Tina and Cheree told her they couldn't fit her in and Cheree told her they didn't have any open appointments this week."

I glanced around the diner, half paying attention as my mind tried to make the jumbled thoughts in my head somewhat organized. The tables were filled and the squeak of the chairs echoed in my head. Ben pushed through the swinging door between the diner and the kitchen with a tray in his hands. He maneuvered his way over to our table and set our food down.

"Doesn't stuff like this happen all the time in those places?" Finn still wasn't buying it. He grabbed the pepper and shook it over his plate. "Gossip. Fights. In ten minutes they're back to being best friends again."

"Y'all need anything else?" Ben asked. "Besides coffee refills?"

"No, I'm good." I picked up the small bowl filled with melted chocolate and poured it over the biscuits instead of using gravy. It was delicious, and I needed some chocolate along with my coffee to think. My eyes zeroed in on my nails and the natural color I'd picked. "Yes," I said to Finn. "But no one usually ends up dead. And Lucy Ellen tried to buy the fingernail polish she wanted painted, but Tina makes her own colors and doesn't sell the polish. That's how Tina has people coming back."

It looked like I was going to have to talk to Tina.

"Maybe she went back there last night." Finn stuck the forkful of food in his mouth.

"Maybe." I shrugged and took a few bites.

I let out a long sigh before taking another drink. I wasn't necessarily frustrated, I just knew that she'd been murdered for the pure fact that Poppa was here and I could see that I was going to have to look into it. "I'm going to have to see what the autopsy says."

I took my phone out of my back pocket and sent Max Bogus a quick text to get me the preliminary autopsy as quickly as possible. My phone rang.

"Oh!" I turned the screen to Finn. "It's Max." I scooted my chair back and hit the talk button before I walked outside and stood on the sidewalk. Poppa and Duke next to me. "Hey, Max. That was quick."

"I got your text and wanted to let you know that Darnell didn't want an autopsy." His words pierced my ears.

"What?" I asked in shock.

"Why would he want to pay for an autopsy when it's pretty certain she died from natural causes?" he said.

"I want an autopsy." I knew that I couldn't order an autopsy if there was no real evidence that pointed to a murder.

"Kenni, I just can't give someone an autopsy because you want it. It's against the law unless you have a reason to think it's a homicide. What's going on?" Max asked with a curious tone.

"Listen, do me a favor." There were some things I wanted to check out before I could point fingers. "Hold off on embalming her until I can get some questions answered."

"He wants her cremated, so that shouldn't be too hard. I can tell him we only cremate certain days. You just let me know how long you need." Max clicked off the phone, letting me know I had a little time to check out what I needed to.

"This might be our hardest one yet." Poppa jumped around like a jumping bean, causing Duke to think he was playing. He barked a few times. "I always loved a good mystery to solve." Poppa rubbed his hands together.

I headed back into the diner. Just as I was about to sit down, my phone rang again. For a hot second I got excited thinking Max had something else to tell me, but that faded when I saw it was Tibbie Bell, one of my best friends.

Finn laughed when I held the phone out to show him who it was.

"Hi, Tibbie." My tone was flat like my enthusiasm for being in Polly's wedding.

"Kenni, I heard Lucy Ellen Lowell is dead, which puts one of the wedding tables out of whack with an odd number of people and that will just upset Polly, but I'm thinking out loud because that's not any concern of yours." I held the phone away from my ear; she was so loud. "I got a call from Polly. She and I were going over the toast for the wedding."

"I'm assuming you don't mean toast you eat?" I joked.

"In a normal situation with you, I'd think that was funny. In Polly's case, not so funny." Her voice was tight, stressed. "Your toast since you're the maid of honor."

"Tibbie." I was going to keep my mouth shut and put on the ugly dress and do my job, but Polly was overstepping the fake friend thing. "You and I are best friends. I would have a lot to say in a toast about you when you decide to get hitched, but Polly? Come on? Can't someone else in her wedding party do it?"

"Don't you think I suggested that, Kenni?" she asked. "Polly insists that you do it. And..." She took too long of a pause.

"What?" I asked with apprehension.

"First thing tomorrow morning I've got a counseling session for you and Polly with Preacher Bing."

"What?" This was getting ridiculous. "Preacher?"

"It's no different than pre-marriage counseling," she said like she was trying to sell me on the idea.

"I'm not marrying Polly Parker." This whole maid-of-honor thing was a big mistake. Huge. "I'm not coming to no counseling with Polly over a fake friendship."

"Kenni, please. This is a big job for me. If I can pull off a wedding for the Parkers, it'll be great for my portfolio. Just do it for me." Tibbie pulled out the big guns.

"I'll only go if you're going to be there too." It was my one stipulation. I wasn't about to do this alone.

"Yes." Suddenly her voice was much happier. "You're the best, Kenni. Be there at seven a.m. It's the only time Preacher had."

"Bring me a coffee. It's the least you can do." I stared over the table at Finn. He was getting money out of his wallet to pay for the food.

"I'll see you at seven a.m. sharp. Don't forget the dress fitting today." Tibbie hung up.

"Are you okay?" Finn's lips turned down and his eyes dropped to the phone in my hand. He looked back up at me. "You don't look happy."

I took the last piece of biscuit and emerged it into the chocolate sauce, then popped it into my mouth.

"Images of me getting stuffed into that dress is something no one should see." I patted my belly and shook my head, rolling my eyes when Finn looked at me with a question in his big brown eyes.

Chapter Six

To everyone else in our small community, life was hunky dory. The wedding was still the talk of the town and a few grumbles about poor Lucy Ellen and her heart attack was all I'd heard during my rounds. Finn and I had said goodbye and he headed back to the department to look through the fax and phone messages that were left overnight. Then there was Betty Murphy, who fielded all the dispatch calls during the day and did small secretarial jobs for us.

Cottonwood was too small to have more than the three of us on staff and during any normal week, there wasn't a murder and this was our routine. This week would seem normal to them until Poppa and I could prove otherwise.

Secretly, I had no other choice but to start looking at possible suspects and Tina Bowers was first on my list. I sat in the Wagoneer in Tiny Tina's parking lot and waited for Tina to turn the sign on the door to OPEN before I interrupted her morning ritual where she got the shop ready for her clients.

"How are we going to get Max to do some sort of toxicology report?" I asked Poppa.

"I haven't figured that out yet." Poppa and I continued to watch the shop door.

My elbow was propped up on the windowsill and my hand

twirled my ponytail, my hairstyle choice for work. It didn't take me long to get ready. With my boyfriend as my coworker, you'd think I'd take a second to get ready by putting on makeup and fixing my hair. But I knew that he'd obviously been attracted to me looking like this, so why alter my appearance? Besides, being sheriff wasn't about being pretty and all girly, though Mama would have me in a pretty gown, heels, and full makeup.

"See what you find out here and then take it from there." He shifted in his seat when Duke jumped to the backseat of the Wagoneer. "What are you trying to accomplish here?"

"I want to see if Tina did Lucy's nails after I left. I know what I heard. There was a roomful of people who could say the exact same thing. I saw what she did with her hand." I slid my finger across my throat. "And then she ends up dead? You and I both know she was murdered. Did Tina do it? She threatened to. But if Tina did do her nails, then maybe she didn't really mean the context of her words and had been just talking."

"You mean gossiping?" Poppa smiled and jerked his head to look at the shop. "What about the other gal in there?"

"Cheree Rath?" Poppa nodded. I said, "I thought about her too. But Lucy Ellen went to Tina. It was Tina that she gave the most grief to." I watched and wondered if Tina Bowers really had it in her to kill someone.

"Not only Tina had a lot to lose from Lucy Ellen going around town and badmouthing everyone. Cheree could lose her job too," Poppa mentioned and adjusted himself in the seat.

"If Tina's business took a nose dive, then there wouldn't be enough customers to have an employee." I looked at Poppa. His brows rose. "Just a thought," I finished.

"One you might want to explore, but I agree that we start with Tina Bowers," he said and pointed to the salon.

Tina flipped the sign on the door to open.

"Let's go," Poppa said before he ghosted out of the Jeep.

I made sure the windows were down, even though it was a cool morning. Duke liked to stick his head out the window.

"Stay," I demanded of Duke and pointed the corner of the *Chronicle* at him before I shut the door.

"Kenni, what are you doing here so early?" Tina fiddled with a clipboard from behind the counter and stuck it on the ledge where customers signed in when they arrived for their appointments.

"Solving a crime. Geez." Poppa's head popped back. "Why do you think?"

He ghosted around the room, darting from one end to the other.

"Two reasons." I wasn't sure if she'd yet heard about Lucy Ellen since it just happened and I wasn't sure she'd seen the paper. I pulled the tucked paper from underneath my arm and set it on the counter with the review facing her. "Have you seen the paper?"

She picked up the *Chronicle* and then set it back down.

"She didn't waste no time," Tina said and pushed the paper a little closer to me. I don't care what she thinks. If she thinks..." She stared at me for a second. "What? What's that look on your face?"

"I had a call from Darnell Lowell around four this morning. He found Lucy Ellen dead when he got home." There was no good way to put it.

"Oh no." Her chest deflated and she gave me a blank stare. "That's awful."

"Are you sure you didn't talk to her since she was here yesterday?" I asked.

"What? You think I had something to do with it?" Her eyes lowered. "You've lost your cotton-pickin' mind."

"Has she? Has she really lost her mind?" Poppa got really close to Tina's face and narrowed his eyes. "I'd say she's doing her job." Poppa glared at Tina.

The phone rang and she grabbed it.

"Tiny Tina's." She did a few mm-hms while flipping through the calendar. "I can reschedule you. Oh." Her eyes slid up to me. She grabbed the paper and took another look. "Fine. Don't call me back when you can't get your nails done somewhere else or when you're in a pinch." She didn't hang the phone up, she smacked it down. "I swear, if she were alive, she wouldn't be for long, because I'd kill her."

The phone rang again.

"Tiny Tina's Salon and Spa. Hi-do, shugs." She smacked her hand on the appointment book. "Mm-hm. I'm sorry you've got to cancel. I'm more than happy to reschedule you for later in the day." She grabbed the pencil, eraser side down, and used it in the appointment book. She grabbed the pencil on both ends and broke it in half. "Ugh!" She threw them on the desk after she hung up the phone.

"I'm guessing that was another cancellation due to the newspaper article?" I asked.

"What the hell is going on?" She spit and gnawed on her lip. "That...that..." She stomped out from behind the counter and threw the paper in the trashcan. "That nasty woman."

"Calm down." I tried to distinguish if she was upset about the cancellation or the article or all of it in general. "Can you tell me where you were last night after you closed the shop?"

"Are you kidding me? Are you kidding me?" she asked as if I hadn't heard her the first time. "You think I killed her?"

"No one said she was murdered." I eyed her suspiciously. "The only reason I ask where you were is because I found it so interesting that she came in here and demanded that you paint her nails and do her hair. You turned her away and when I went there this morning, her nails were painted Perfectly Posh."

"Not my Perfectly Posh." She drew her hand up to her chest. "I only have one bottle and don't make more until I'm out."

"What if you run out?" I questioned.

"Then I go right back there and whip more up," she said and gestured to the back room.

Tina darted from her station to Cheree's station, picking through the bottles of nail polish.

"Where in tarnation is it?" Her eyes darted around the room before they settled on mine. "It's not here. She stole it!" Her face grew red as her hand fisted at her side. "She stole it when she was here yesterday and I wasn't looking."

She went from station to station, through every drawer, tearing up the place.

"Listen." I stuck my hand out and tried to stop her. She was frantically looking under, in, and around every nook and cranny in the salon. "If she came back later in the day and you did her nails, it's fine. I just need you to tell me."

"I'm telling you right now that I didn't call her. The last time I saw her was when you saw her." She stomped her foot and pointed down to the floor. "Right here in this very spot."

"Did Cheree have her come back in?" There had to be an answer to this strange situation.

"Not that I know of. Cheree left before I did. It was my late night." She darted off toward the back of the shop. "I'm going to look back here just in case Cheree put it back by the color lab."

"Color lab?" I asked.

"It's where I make my color magic for my polishes like the one Lucy Ellen stole right from underneath my nose!" She hollered before she disappeared through the hippie hanging plastic beads that substituted for a door.

While she looked in the back room, I took a stroll around the salon. The two massaging chairs for the pedicures were clean and ready for the next customer. Between them was a small table with tabloids from two years ago. The cabinet on rolling wheels that Cheree and Tina brought over to finish up the pedicures was tucked neatly behind them.

I rolled it out and looked at the colors on top and the jars with blue cleaner. The pedicure tools were emerged in them. When I didn't see the distinctive nail color, I pulled out the top drawer and found the spongey things they put between toes. The second drawer was the packages of flip-flops they supplied and the third drawer was filled with cotton balls.

After I rolled the pedicure cart back where I'd found it, I walked over to Cheree's nail station. On the right side of the table were the few nail colors that were on display. There was a black folded towel on each side of the table where the customer's hands rested while Cheree filed, trimmed, and painted. On the left side of the table was the acrylic nail light where the customer put her hands in the glowing tube for the nails to dry. I'd never done those; I was more of the naked nail kind of gal, but not Lucy. Her nails were as fake as could be.

In the drawers were new nail files and all the ingredients that were used for the acrylic nails. There wasn't anything different on Tina's side. Then there was the front desk. Besides the register, there was a landline phone, an appointment book, and a fake plant.

In front of the desk were two wire lawn chairs and a small table with more tabloid magazines that were just as old as the ones by the pedicure chairs.

I picked up the cordless phone and almost hit the redial button, but noticed there was a caller ID screen. I used the left arrow to scroll through and there was Lucy's name along with her phone number. Lucy Ellen did say that she'd called earlier that day and the timestamp did go with her story.

"Did the phone ring?" Tina came back in the shop with a fist full of glass polish bottles. "I couldn't find it, but I did have these that I can use in its place until I can make more up."

She held up a bottle with pink polish, but not the exact same color.

"No." I hung the phone back up. "I was looking to see your caller ID."

"Kenni, you're making me feel like I've done something wrong. Is there something you need to tell me?" she asked.

The phone rang.

"Hold that thought." She put her finger with a dagger-like nail up in a hold-on gesture. "Tiny Tina's, best sal-lon and spa in Cottonwood."

Her accent made "salon" sound like two separate words and she did leave out the fact that she was the only salon and spa in Cottonwood so it was automatically the best.

"I heard she died." Tina twisted her piece of gum around her finger and planted her hiney up against the front desk with her back facing the front. "Mm-hm. Heart attack? She came in here yesterday all wound up tight. No wonder." Tina nodded her head like the person on the other end could see her. "Poor girl. From what I heard, she was knock-kneed when she was little and I bet that's what made her crazy as a June bug." She stood silent for a minute. "That was ridiculous. I saw it and I can't believe that after all these years she decided to give me a bad review. And you know, people won't remember her for her. When her name comes up, they'll remember this mean review."

About that time the front door opened and the bell that was bread-tied on the arm of the hardware of the door jingled. The customer sat down in one of the lawn chairs, waiting for Tina to get off the phone.

"Listen, I've got to go, but put me down for some deviled eggs." She stopped talking, then picked right back up. "I am bringing something. I don't care if she didn't like me as of the time of this paper hitting the streets. She was a client of mine for two years. I know her deepest, darkest secrets." Tina hung up.

"Deepest, darkest secrets?" Poppa and I asked at the same time.

"When you sit your tushie in that chair, it's like getting a shot of truth serum," she snarled. "Right now I'm not ready to talk about the dead when her body isn't even cold."

"Something to remember when you drag her in for questioning." Poppa eyed Tina.

"What about deviled eggs?" I asked and decided to let the darkest-secret thing go until Max confirmed that Lucy Ellen was murdered. Then it was fair game to press Tina for answers.

"They're getting together the repast for Lucy Ellen's funeral, though they don't know when Darnell is going to have it." She gave a simple shrug and pulled a black apron off the back of the chair and tied it around her waist. "Hon," she got the customer's attention, "you ready?"

The customer got up and headed on back to the manicure station.

"If you find that bottle of nail polish let me know." I put my hand on the door.

"I'll see you Thursday," she said.

"Thursday?" I turned and questioned with the door partially opened, wondering if the funeral had already been planned.

"Mmm-hmm." She nodded with pinched lips. "Tibbie Bell left a message on the machine and said you're stepping in to be

Polly's number one and she's got the sal-lon booked for nails on Thursday."

"Yeah. See you Thursday," I muttered and left the salon with a feeling that I'd be back real soon with more questions.

"Polly," I groaned and remembered the dress fitting Tibbie had scheduled for me. "We've got to get you to the station." I rubbed Duke's head before I shoved him to the backseat of the Jeep.

"Where are we going?" Poppa asked. "Camille Shively's I hope, because you've got to find out about that stuff Darnell was spouting off about Lucy's health and we've got to prove she wasn't sick so we can get him to agree to an autopsy."

"That might be a good angle." I never thought about getting Camille on my side. "I'm not sure how forthcoming she'll be with information regarding Lucy Ellen and I know I won't be able to get a warrant for Lucy's records on a just-because-I-want-to-see excuse to the judge. No judge will give me that warrant."

Camille Shively wasn't one of my friends in school. She was a little younger than me, but old enough to be the new doctor in town now that our former baby doctor was no longer among the living.

"Somehow someway you've got to figure out how we can get an autopsy on that body before Max cremates it. Speaking of the dead." Poppa pointed to my left over to the Old Cemetery, the only graveyard in Cottonwood and his final resting place along with everyone else's. "I better go check up on my friends." Poppa ghosted off just as the first light of the three on Main Street turned red.

Chapter Seven

Duke jumped up in the front seat and stuck half of his body out the window. His tongue hanging out of his mouth made his slobber fling up on the windshield. I watched as Poppa's ghost crossed Main Street and floated along the old limestone slave wall that surrounded the cemetery. The walls were historically preserved and couldn't be touched. They were built by Irish immigrants and they could be found all over the state of Kentucky.

When the light turned green, we drove south on Main Street. The Sweet Adelines had been busy this morning hanging up new banners on all the dowel rods from the carriage lights that dotted Main Street on both sides. The summer baskets of flowers provided by Myrna Savage's Petal Pushers Florist had been replaced with new baskets filled with mums of a variety of reds, oranges, and yellows. It was the perfect flower choice for the between-seasons décor.

Kentucky in the autumn was a beautiful place; if only the death of Lucy Ellen Lowell wasn't hanging over my head I'd have enjoyed the drive to the office that much more. Normally I'd take a right off of Main and pull down the alley in front of the department, but there was a prime parking spot in front of Cowboy's Catfish Restaurant. I jerked the wheel and pulled right on in.

Cowboy's Catfish had the best catfish and hushpuppies around. And it just so happened that the sheriff's department rented the room behind Cowboy's from owner Bartleby Fry. It was cheaper for Cottonwood to rent the room than building and running our own one-cell facility. The only job hazard was smelling the home-cooked food. Today's special was Kentucky round steak, also known as fried bologna. Duke and I loved nothing better than a piece of fried bologna with mustard between two slices of white bread and a side of Bartleby's sliced potatoes and onions.

"My oh my." I rubbed my belly when I walked into the front door of the restaurant. "Something sure does smell good."

It was good to see all the tables in use and the dining room filled with conversations.

Duke trotted back to the kitchen where he knew he was in for a treat.

"Why is it that you always walk in that front door when I'm cooking up bologna?" Bartleby laughed when I passed him on the way to the department.

"Luck, I guess." I winked and opened the door of the office where Betty Murphy was sitting at her desk talking on the phone. "Come on, Duke." I patted my leg and shut the door after he meandered in. "Oh, stop pouting."

I walked over to Finn's desk and grabbed a dog treat out of the tin sitting there as Betty hung up her call.

"I sure did hate to hear about Lucy Ellen this morning." Betty looked up from filing her nails. "She sure will be missed at bell choir."

"Bell choir?" I asked.

"Yeah." Betty looked up over her glasses. "She's a member of the First Baptist Church bell choir. She's our gyro handbellist."

"Handbellist?" I questioned if that was a word, but went with it anyway. "What is a gyro?"

"It's the vibration of the bell when held in a certain position and gives a different ring than just fluidly ringing the bell. There's so many techniques." Betty held her hand in the air and pretended as if she were ringing her handbell.

"Isn't Blanche Bailey a member of the bell choir?" I asked about the lady who did all the alterations in town and just so happened to be doing my Scarlett O'Hara dress fitting.

I wasn't the best church-going gal in Cottonwood. Making sure that all the fine citizens of our community and their property were safe while they were in church was the great excuse I gave Preacher on why I wasn't able to attend on a regular basis.

"She sure is. She's getting our Christmas Cantata ready." A worried look crossed her face. "Oh dear," her brows furrowed, "I'm not sure who's going to take Lucy's spot since she was our only gyro and the crowd goes nuts over that. And to think the women of the Hunt Club are doing the annual gun show without her."

"I'm sure Blanche will have all of that worked out." I glanced up at the clock over top of the one cell and noticed by the time I got home, grabbed my dress, and got to Blanche's house, it'd be time for my fitting. "Speaking of Blanche, I've got a dress fitting."

"I heard all about you doing that silly maid-of-honor thingy while I was at Lulu's Boutique this morning when I stopped to get breakfast from Jolee's food truck." Betty's face softened into a smile. "Your mama was asking everyone to pray that you'd catch the wedding bouquet."

"That would just make Mama's year, wouldn't it?" I asked.

Out of nowhere, I imagined me standing in that ugly dress watching the bouquet of flowers floating toward me, hitting me in the head and falling to my feet when I refused to catch it.

Right then I vowed not to even participate in the stupid tradition. I'd already compromised my values to be in the wedding (and by agreeing to wear the ugly dress in front of all Cottonwood), but to give an inkling that I was ready to walk down the aisle by catching some silly bouquet that was attached to an old wives' tale? Forget it.

"Do you mind keeping an eye on Duke?" I asked Betty, since he was all curled up and sleeping on his bed near my desk. "I won't be long."

"You know I don't mind." She smiled at him like everyone did when they looked at the big lug. "He keeps me company. And he keeps the best secrets." She winked.

I shook my head, grabbed my bag, and headed back through Cowboy's Catfish, but not without stopping and popping a hushpuppy in my mouth.

"I'll have a plate for y'all in the department when you get back," Bartleby called through the chattering crowd.

I gave him the two-finger toodles on my way out the front door since my mouth was stuffed with the delicious golden crispy ball of dough.

Blanche lived on Second Street. It was only a couple of blocks over from the department. There was a small creek that ran alongside Second Street and all the houses. Each house had a small bridge going over the creek that connected the road and the driveway. It was just another cozy feature of Cottonwood that made the small town so lovely to live in.

I double checked the address Polly Parker had given me because there were several cars in the drive and the last thing I wanted to do was to try a dress on in front of anyone. Being a few minutes early, I'd decided to give Darnell Lowell a quick call and check up on him as well as throw in the question about Lucy's health.

"Hi, Darnell. It's Kenni Lowry." I didn't say Sheriff because I felt that saying my name without the title was a lot less formal. When I didn't have my uniform on, people saw me as a regular person and didn't worry about what they were saying around me. "How are you doing?"

"I'm just not sure what I'm going to do." He didn't sound any better than he had in the wee hours of the morning. "I just feel like she's gone to one of her meetin's this morning and will be home directly."

"Again, I'm so sorry for your loss." I wasn't sure how I was going to get him to even think about an autopsy when he wasn't even accepting that she was gone. "As sheriff, I do need to make sure that you are positive you don't want an autopsy to find out exactly how she died."

"I just figured it was a heart attack. I mean, she'd been going to see Dr. Shively and all. Lucy Ellen said she was seeing stars. Like shooting stars. One of the women down at Tiny Tina's told her that shooting stars meant high blood pressure. Then she came home with some little pills after her doctor's appointment." I could hear an uncertain tone in his voice. Maybe I was getting to him.

"And wouldn't you like to know for sure that Lucy Ellen had high blood pressure and that's what killed her? I mean, I don't want you to beat yourself up over it for years wondering." I crossed my fingers, squeezed my eyes together, and gave a little prayer that he'd change his mind.

"I never thought of it like that." There was a hesitation. "I don't know, Kenni. I just want to let her rest in peace. We are firm believers that when it's your time to go, it's your time to go."

My phone beeped. I pulled it away from my ear and looked at the screen to see who was calling in.

"Darnell, I've got to go, but you think about it. I just want to make sure that you're doing okay and since you don't have any children, I wanted to offer my suggestion. I'll check in on you later." I didn't wait for his response. I clicked over. "Hey, Max. It doesn't look like I'm going to get Darnell to change his mind about an autopsy."

"Sheriff, it doesn't look like you have to," Max said. "I started inputting all of Lucy's information into the database to register for the death certificate. Lucy Ellen popped up as a certified organ donor. I'm not sure even Darnell knows that."

"And? Are you trying to tell me that you found something out?" I asked.

"All of her organs looked pretty healthy and when I ran the preliminary tests to start to register them...Well." He hesitated. "I'm not sure how you knew, but none of her organs are viable. She's full of poison."

"Poison?" I asked.

Out of the corner of my eye, I could see Poppa appear in the passenger seat.

His round checks were puffing out with a big smile on his face, his comb-over was neatly splayed across the top of his head, and his sheriff uniform was just as pressed and pristine as it was the days he wore it.

"Cyanide, to be exact." Max's words were music to my ears.

"Cyanide?" It was like we were in a repeating game. There was really no reason for me to be shocked, but I was. It was wrapping around me, making me feel like I needed air. Lots of air. I rolled down the window and let the breeze fill the Wagoneer with fresh air as I took a few deep breaths.

"It looks like she died between seven p.m. and four a.m. You've got another homicide on your hands. If you want to stop by, I've got a copy of the organ report. I'm going to call Darnell to let him know that I've turned the case over to you, if that's okay?" Max asked.

"Yeah. Of course it's okay. Listen, I've got to run into Blanche Bailey's and try on a dress for her. I'll stop by after that." I stared at Poppa and slowly shook my head.

Max laughed.

"I heard you're the new maid of honor for the Parker girl's wedding." He laughed harder.

"Word sure does travel fast around here," I noted.

"Yep. And I better get off the phone. Do you want me to call Darnell?" He asked.

"You know what." I hesitated because I should've probably told him, but now Darnell had no choice but to accept the autopsy. It was one last step I had to worry about. "I do want you to call Darnell and tell him that I asked you to call him and we are moving forward with a full autopsy."

"Sounds good. Well, I need to get back to finding out the source of this poisoning. I'll see you soon." Max clicked off the phone.

"Weeee doggie." Poppa smacked his leg. "Go on. Get out of here. We've got a murder to solve."

"I wish I could. I've got to get in there and have Blanche fit me in this dress. It'll give Max time to call Darnell about Lucy." I gnawed on my bottom lip. "And some time for him to process it. Now my questions for him and Tina Bowers are much different."

"Don't forget Jolee Fischer had words with Lucy Ellen too." Poppa knew that Jolee was my friend, but to be fair we questioned anyone and everyone. "Everyone's a suspect until we get the real killer."

I looked down at my phone and used the pad of my thumb to scroll to Finn's name. I hit send.

"Hey there." Finn was always so chipper when I called.

"You won't sound so happy when I tell you that Lucy Ellen Lowell was murdered." I turned the Wagoneer off and reached behind me, dragging that godawful green dress to the front seat. "Max Bogus just called. He said that when he put Lucy's information into the computer to generate the death certificate, she popped up as an organ donor. Long story short, her organs are poisoned with cyanide."

"You called it." Finn didn't seem as surprised as I thought he would. "I don't know how you do it, but you can spot a murdered victim in a second flat upon arrival to a scene."

"Maybe one day I'll tell you my secret," I said, looking over at Poppa.

"No you won't either," Poppa warned.

"What can I do?" he asked.

"I've actually got to go into Blanche Bailey's to try on this maid-of-honor dress for Polly's wedding. After that I'm going to go grab the report from Max and head back to the office to open the official homicide investigation." There were definitely some things he could do that would help. "Max said he was going to call Darnell and turn the case over to us. Do you think you can head back over to the Lowell place and secure the scene? We have to scour that entire house."

I was never so glad that I took photos than I was right now.

"I can do that." He was so agreeable.

"And I also want you to go ask Jolee about her confrontation with Lucy." There was no way I wanted to question Jolee. It was a conflict of interest. "She said something about her and Lucy Ellen having an argument over the food at Polly's wedding or something. I really can't recall because it was when I was at Tiny Tina's and they were all gossiping about everything."

I wished I'd listened better now.

"That's a tough situation to be in with your best friend." He wasn't telling me anything I didn't already know.

"That's why I want you to interview her. Not that I think she did it, but I feel like I need to question everyone who Lucy Ellen had words with." It was only logical.

Back issues of the *Cottonwood Chronicle* would help me figure out who all those people were since Lucy Ellen was so good at writing negative reviews. The library would have all the back issues.

"Then your best friend is going to hate me. That's the last thing I want as your boyfriend." Him just saying that made me tingly. "I do love you."

"I love you too. So maybe we can get together at your place tonight since we always go to mine." It was a simple suggestion, but I loved his new addition and comfy couch. "A night of Netflix and some snuggling. Of course with Duke and Cosmo." I had to throw in the fur babies.

"Kenni Lowry, you're sweet talking me into going to talk to Jolee." The hint of sexy teasing made me giggle.

"Is it working?" I asked.

"I can't wait. I'll even grab us a couple of plates of food from her food truck." That was a great plan. "I'll text you when I get finished securing the Lowell house."

"Be sure to tell Darnell that we need him to stay somewhere else tonight." I almost forgot that he couldn't be there. Not that the place wasn't probably already tainted from him there, but at least I'd taken some photos. "Talk soon."

"Sounds good." He clicked off before me. I smiled. Suddenly going to try on the nasty green dress in my grip didn't seem so bad knowing that Finn was going to be next to me all night.

"Really? Your mama and daddy were never that goo-goo over each other." Poppa rolled his eyes. "We've got to stay focused. Keep our eye on the prize. The killer. Cottonwood isn't safe."

"First, I've still got to live life, and that includes this dress and my relationship with Finn." My brows rose. "Cottonwood is safe. Lucy Ellen Lowell had a lot more enemies than anyone realized. She made someone mad and that's who's killed her. You and I will figure it out like we always do."

"That's not how we did things when I was sheriff." Poppa was old school and I knew that.

"Poppa, you're here to help me. I'm the sheriff now, and right now we have to let Max do his job and figure out how he thinks she got the poison. There's nothing we can do until her body talks to him. In the meantime, we'll pay Tina another visit."

Poppa must've hated my answer because he ghosted away.

"Oh well." The green dress was flapping in the wind behind me on my way up to Blanche's door. I jumped back when she flung the door open.

"We've been waiting for you," she trilled and swung one arm out. "Tibbie called."

There was an elastic snap attached to her wrist and she wore a bright yellow-and-orange-swirl caftan. Her red hair flowed down her back. Her big brown eyes shone and a smile curled up on the edges of her lips. She took a step back for me to enter.

If there was one thing that Blanche was, it was eccentric. She was in so many women's groups because the word on the street was that the women in Cottonwood liked to know where

Blanche was at all times. She was a flirt and she didn't care who she flirted with. The women wanted to keep her close to them.

"Who's been waiting for me?" I asked and stepped into the red walls of her lair.

"The girls from bell choir." She dragged her long fingers down her hair. There was a smirk on her face. She reached out. "I'll take that." She plucked the dress from my hands.

"And why have they been waiting for me?" I asked.

"Do come on in." She walked down the hall and opened a door. "You can go in here and try on the dress. When you are ready, just walk down the hallway and you'll find us."

She hooked the dress on a coat tree inside the room. The room had three sewing machines and all three looked to be in use with something stuck to the needle. There was a rack of clothes and tags with names written on each one. Blanche was a busy woman.

After I'd gotten my sheriff's uniform off, I unzipped the curtain...er...dress and slipped it on. I could barely reach the zipper so I left what I couldn't reach. The murmuring and whispers spilled out and down the hall, leading me right to the women. This room was painted red too. There was a black fireplace that literally hung from the ceiling. It was the strangest thing I'd ever seen. There was a low flame that had to have been set for ambiance. The sweet songs of Frank Sinatra spilled from the ceiling speakers.

On the couch sat Mama, Myrna Savage, Ruby Smith, Viola White, and Dr. Camille Shively with big smiles on their faces.

"Tea?" Blanche dramatically swung her hand across a three-tiered plate filled with cookies and other sweet treats. "Cookie?"

"Well, hello," I said in a flat voice.

Mama jumped up.

"Let me zip you the rest of the way up." She hurried behind me.

"Oh, you look so lovely. *Gone with the Wind*." Camille's shoulders and edges of her mouth lifted in a delighted gesture before she stuffed a cookie in her mouth.

"Don't you have patients?" I asked, wondering how I was going to slip in some questions about Lucy's health, though it really didn't matter now that her death had gone from natural to homicide. I was still curious.

"I get a lunch." She eased back in the folds of the couch. "Besides, I wouldn't've missed seeing you in that dress for the world after I heard you were filling in."

If I'd not pushed all the air out of my lungs to try and get this dress zipped up, I would've protested.

"If you could just get it over her bottom rib, you can tug real hard." Viola White gave her two cents before she jumped up, pushing her big round black glasses upon the edge of her nose. "Let me try."

"Really?" My brows rose.

"Suck up and in." Viola's head jerked around my right shoulder to look at me so she knew I heard what she said. Her bright red lipstick gave a pop of color to her pasty white skin and short, spikey red hair.

"I'm sucking in the best I can." I filled my lungs again.

She jerked, and red feathers on her vest flew through the air.

"Pfft. Pfft," I blew as the feathers floated down and got close to my mouth.

"Honey, you might be happy it don't fit. I mean, the color." Viola gave up. She came around to look at the front of the dress. Her fingers played with the multi-beaded necklace that draped her neckline under the vest. "I love color. It gives a little life. In fact, color can raise the dead, but this color won't raise no one."

"Mmmhmm." Ruby Smith nodded and agreed. Her lips and hair matched Viola's red feathery vest. Her lips pursed. "Ugly."

"Move it, Viola." Mama practically shoved Viola out of the way. She tugged the dress a little further up on my waist and walked behind me.

"This is my daughter's time to shine in a dress in front of Cottonwood. I'm not giving up that easily." Mama tugged on the zipper and jutted me forward a few times.

"Mama, you're hurting me." I cringed.

"Fashion hurts." Viola White always wore the awfulest-looking get-ups she claimed were high fashion. Since she was the wealthiest woman in Cottonwood, she should know.

Mama whispered something so low I couldn't understand her.

"Huh?" I asked and jerked as the zipper pierced my skin with another jerk.

She mumbled so I still couldn't hear her.

"What?" I asked again.

"Suck in!" she hollered with a follow up of gasps from the peanut gallery. "More!"

"Honey." Blanche tsked, walking slowly around me. Her eyes focused on the dress or maybe the skin that was trying to get stuffed in the dress. My skin. "Looks like someone's gained a little weight." She winked at me. "Happy weight."

I sucked in.

"Try it again, Mama." No way had I gained weight.

When I felt Mama start to tug, I sucked in real deep this time because the look on all of those henny-hen faces was my signal that my not being able to fit into the dress was going to be the hot topic of gossip. Forget about Lucy Ellen Lowell dying. Mama sucked in too and held her breath.

"Nuh-uh." Mama let go, the air leaving her body. "It's not going to zip." There was a bit of disappointment in her tone.

"Yes. Happy fat." Blanche did another walk around me.

This time there was a yellow measuring tape dangling around her neck like a scarf and a pincushion in the shape of a tomato clipped around her wrist with all sorts of pins stuck in it.

"Happy fat?" I wasn't sure, but I think Blanche Bailey just called me fat. "There's no such thing."

Was there? I looked at Camille.

"This is just an old dress that's not the right size." I sucked in so much that I nearly passed out.

"Nope. Not going to zip." Mama's face had a look of concern. "Can you add fabric?" She turned to Blanche.

"Mmmhmm." Blanche nodded and ho-hummed behind pinched lips. "That's happy fat for sure. It's what we get when we are in love. So you must be in love with that handsome Finn Vincent."

"Not that northerner. No way. Ain't that right, Kenni?" Myrna Savage's eyes focused on the dress.

"Love doesn't put fat on you." It was ridiculous. "Right, Camille?"

Camille looked up over her tea cup. She took a quick sip and set it on the saucer on the coffee table in front of her.

"It's not a real term, but I have heard that when we are happy, we tend to gain a little weight, but that's just from some silly study. I didn't read it because you still look good and as your doctor, I'd tell you if I was concerned."

"I'm sure concerned," Mama griped.

"Alright." I turned and headed back down the hall. "I'm out of here."

"Viv! What's wrong with you?" I heard Blanche say to Mama. "She's not only a wonderful woman, but she's an amazing sheriff and girlfriend.”

I shut the room door that Blanche used as the dressing room for her sewing business. I turned around, my reflection was staring back at me from the mirrored closet doors. The green dress did nothing for me. I swear the movie version was much more romantic than the real version and surely to goodness Polly Parker didn't think this dress was pretty.

“Easy for you to say. You've got a daughter who's married and gave you grandchildren. I'm beginning to think Kenni is allergic to being a wife. She wants to go around packing a gun all day and chasing bad guys.” Mama did the same song and dance with them as she did me.

“She looks great. You're gonna run that girl off one day,” Myrna warned. “And you complain that she doesn't stop by and see you all the time. Well, I wouldn't either if you talked about me like that.”

I turned around and looked at the backside. There wasn't much more room for the zipper to be zipped. Happy fat? Who ever heard of such a thing?

“Maybe I do, behind your back,” Mama teased Myrna.

“Speaking of gossip.” Myrna's voice caught my attention. “Can y'all believe that Lucy Ellen is dead?”

“Such a shame, and at a young age.” Blanche's voice and footsteps were coming closer to the dressing room. There was a slight knock on the door. “Kenni, can I come in?”

I took one last look in the mirrored closet doors and with a deep sigh, walked over to the door and opened it.

“Come on in,” I said flatly. “Happy fat? Really?”

“Honey, it's no big deal. You'll lose it. I see that boy stare at you when I'm at Ben's eating breakfast. You don't even notice me because you're so goo-goo over him.” She smiled. There was a twinkle in her eye. “I wish I had that kind of love. All them women think I'm trying to steal their men, but I'm not. I just like a little attention." She winked and planted a hand on each of my shoulders. She turned me around to look in the mirrors. "You know what I see?"

I shook my head and looked at her as she peered over my shoulder.

"I see a strong, independent woman that never let anyone stop her from getting what she wanted. Including Finn Vincent." She grinned ear to ear. "All them single girls out there nearly fell all over each other trying to court him. He only had eyes for you. I could see it. Besides, this dress is ugly and the fabric doesn't give. I have no idea what Polly Parker was thinking."

I laughed and pushed my shoulders back.

"Chance Ryland is no Rhett Butler." Her brows rose and she winked. She patted my shoulders. "Now, let me get this pinned all together and I'll have it ready in no time. And..." She looked me square in the eyes. "Between me and you, that girl Polly had as a maid of honor, I bet she saw this dress and immediately backed out." Her fingernail tapped my chest. "You've got a heart of gold. I know you and Polly aren't friends, but that's your nature. A giving spirit. Don't you listen to your mama."

Blanche Bailey should've been a therapist. I left that room feeling better than I had in years. There wasn't anything stopping me from confronting Mama and the other women as they sipped their teas and gossiped about Lucy.

"We've got it all taken care of," Blanche said and headed back to the chaise lounge in the corner of the family room. Her caftan billowed out around her before she sat down. "Now, what was it you were saying about Lucy Ellen Lowell?"

"Myrna was talking about how Kenni was dispatched to their house this morning when Darnell got home and found her dead of an apparent heart attack." Mama had no problems

telling my business. Her mantra was what was mine was hers
and what was hers was hers.

My eyes lowered when I looked at Myrna. She turned her
face and chin away from my glare. I knew she could see me even
from the dimly lit room that was lit up from a dangling light that
was red with gold flecks. Blanche Bailey sure did love red.

"I have a po-lice scanner." Myrna crossed her arms. "Ain't
nothing illegal about that."

"Camille, Darnell told me that she just came to see you last
week. Was she ill? Such a shame," I said, adding the last part for
good measure.

I took the tea Blanche had poured for me and sat down in
one of the chairs.

"She had claimed she was seeing stars, you know, like from
high blood pressure. I gave her a machine to wear and nothing
ever registered." She let out a long sigh of sadness. "She was
healthy as far as I could tell. Sometimes freak heart attacks
happen."

"You didn't give her any meds?" I asked.

"I'd have to look in her chart, but I could've told her to take
a vitamin or baby aspirin or something." She shrugged.

"She didn't die of a heart attack." Gingerly, I brought my tea
up to my lips and took a sip, enjoying the dropped jaws and
popped open eyes staring back at me. These women weren't just
part of the bell choir, they were the hiney hens of Cottonwood.
What I meant by that: they were the gossip central to all things
worth gossiping about. Like my Poppa taught me, there's a little
bit of truth in all gossip. If I kept my ear to the rumblings, I just
might get some information or leads to check out. Especially
about people who had something against Lucy Ellen Lowell.
Because any lead right now was a welcomed one.

"She was poisoned. I'm now investigating it as a murder." I

set the cup down on the table. "Which reminds me. I've got some people I need to talk to."

"People?" Myrna asked in a silky voice and leaned forward. All the henny-hens, the gossiping women in the room, focused on me. "As in who?" Myrna shifted her legs to the side and took a sip of her tea as if she weren't as interested as she really was.

"People that might've had a beef with her." I shrugged and looked down into my tea while I took a sip so I could let them look between themselves without them thinking I saw them.

"Did you check the men in the hunt club?" Ruby Smith asked.

"What about them?" This was exactly what I wanted to happen when I told them Lucy Ellen had been murdered.

"You know when people walk around the shop, they talk to one another." Ruby was the owner of Ruby's Antiques on Main Street. "If they bring in a big piece like a sideboard or something, they usually bring one of the members of the club because they need help carrying it."

"Did you hear something from one of them?" I asked and took a sip.

"I overheard a couple of them talking about how Lucy Ellen had taken some cash that belonged to the club and Darnell said that he was going to replace it because Lucy Ellen thought it was their money. But you know men." She sighed and raised a sly brow. "The hunt club men." She looked at all the women in the room and they all were nodding and agreeing, which kept the gossip going. "They like to know exactly where their money is going."

"I wonder if that's what Bosco and Darnell got into a fight about?" Viola asked. "That's just hearsay from Alma Frederick when she came in to get that no-good diamond he got her." She rolled her eyes, magnified under those big glasses. She owned

White's Jewelry in Main Street across from Ruby's Antiques. "I told Bosco that it might be big, but the quality of the diamond wasn't the best." She laughed. "He said that she'd never know because she only wanted a big one that made all the women in the hunt club jealous."

"Why do you keep that trash in your shop?" Mama asked.

"Because people that can't afford the nicer cuts and quality do like to show off a little. I have to cater to everyone." Viola sucked in a deep breath. "Bosco Frederick can afford a good diamond. After all the crap Alma has put up with all these years."

"What did Alma put up with?" I asked.

Viola looked at me. Her eyes narrowed and glanced over my uniform. Darn. The darn uniform always stopped everyone from talking to me. It was the strangest thing. I could've had that dress on and Viola's lips would've been flapping with information.

"Honey, it's all a little gossip that don't matter a hill of beans. Well, phooey." She scrunched up her nose when she looked at her watch. She sat her tea on the table and grabbed her purse. "I've got to get going."

"I better get back to work too," Camille spoke up and tapped her watch. "My lunch hour is over." She grabbed her purse and hustled down the hallway.

"You call me!" Mama hollered after Camille.

"And I've got flowers for Lucy's service to get ready." Myrna stood up and brushed her hands down her shirt. "I'll talk to you gals later."

My job here was done. I'd put the bug in their ears. They weren't going to go do any work. Camille was going to go back to the office to gossip, while Myrna was probably going to call the people who bought flowers and tell them about the murder.

Viola was going to question everyone that came in her jewelry shop about the murder and if they didn't know, she'd be more than happy to claim hearsay so it didn't appear like she was gossiping. I'd given them enough gossip to go forth and do some of my investigation for me.

It'd churn up some details on who just might've fought with Lucy Ellen other than Tina and Jolee.

Why on earth would they really kill her after they'd jokingly threatened her in front of me, the sheriff?

Most of the gossip was a lot of hot air. But my process got down to the truth. I took what was said in the gossip and whittled it down. The truth usually ended up being about half of the gossip. Still, gossip gave me leads and leads led me to questions and questioning people. It was something I'd learned from Poppa.

"I guess I better go. Now that my happy fat will fit into the dress." There wasn't any sort of alarming tone in my voice, just satisfaction that I'd given them the shock of their lives. "Blanche, you're better than any therapist out there."

Mama shot a look at Blanche that was filled with daggers.

"Mama, good to see you." I cordially nodded at both of them.

"Choo, choo." Poppa appeared next to Mama. "You've got the gossip train on a roll. Now we let that get going and sit back to listen in. There's a little truth in each bit of gossip. We've just got to find it."

Chapter Eight

The morgue was located in the basement of Cottonwood Funeral Home, the only funeral home in our town, and no matter how many bodies I'd seen, it never got any easier standing in the door of the cold institutional-looking room staring at the dead body lying on the stainless-steel table. Especially when you knew the person.

"You gonna pass out?" Max Bogus gestured to the yellow paper gown hanging on the coat rack for me to put on over my clothes.

"Nah." I put my arms through the holes of the yellow gown and wrapped the ties around my waist. I plucked a couple of gloves from the cardboard box and snapped them on my hands. "Anything new?"

"Yeah." He nodded his round face. He stared at me behind his thick-rimmed glasses from over Lucy's body. A scalpel in one hand and a magnifying glass in the other. "You aren't going to believe this."

"Try me." I took my time walking over and stopped a few feet away from the table.

"A large portion of the cyanide is around her fingers, mainly her nail base." He pointed to Lucy's hand with the scalpel. "I scraped a piece of the nail polish off and ran a quick test. Full of the poison."

"You're telling me that Lucy Ellen died from cyanide poisoning in fingernail polish?" I asked, knowing this was the nail in Tina's coffin if that was the case.

"That's exactly what I'm saying." He took a step back and put the items on the rolling tray next to the autopsy table. He took the gloves off, throwing them in the hazardous waste bin along with the yellow gown, and motioned for me to follow him to his office. "Of course, this was a quick preliminary test. I've sent a large sample off to the lab so we can get the breakdowns that I need to finish the report up."

I took off my gloves and gown, putting them on the counter in case I needed to put them back on since they weren't really used and followed him into the office, which was just through another door.

He tucked his blue button-down shirt further into his khaki pants before he sat down in the office chair behind his desk. The room was simple, nothing fancy. He had a desk full of paper piles and a chair in front of his desk, which was where I sat. On the wall were his medical license, business license, and coroner's license. He only had up the necessary items to prove who he was in case he was audited.

Max lived a simple life. He went to work, did his job, and enjoyed his home in the country. There wasn't any romance or social life that I knew of, but then again, I didn't stay in the gossip groups.

"I've seen a lot in my time, but this takes the cake." He opened a file and set it in front of me. He pointed to numbers and graphs that told me about the levels of poison and what they meant.

Of course, the only thing I cared about was the signed

autopsy report that stated the cause of death as homicide by poison, because it gave me the go-ahead to start an official investigation.

"If you can find the bottle of nail polish, I bet you'll find the murder weapon." He peeled the glasses off of his face and dropped them on this desk. His elbows rested on the arms of his chair after he eased back and clasped his hands, resting them on his belly. "I never ever thought I'd say nail polish was a murder weapon."

"Unfortunately," it made me sick thinking about it, much less saying it, "Tina Bowers is my number one suspect."

"How did you come to that conclusion?" he asked.

"Yesterday I was at Tiny Tina's cashing in a gift certificate." I left out the details of how Finn had made me take a day off. This was business, not a social call. Nor did he care why I was at Tiny Tina's. "Lucy Ellen came in all upset because Tina wouldn't make her a hair appointment or fit her in for her nails. When she left, Tina said she probably should've cut her hair but let the shears slip across her neck."

"She said that?" His brows furrowed.

"And she did this." I slid my finger across my throat like Tina had done.

"But none of that makes sense." Poppa appeared behind Max. "You don't tell on yourself when you're planning on murdering someone."

"That's strange." Max sat up. "If that's the case, it could be premeditated murder." He reached over and shut the file. "But that's for you to figure out."

It would definitely be premeditated if Tina had gone to the trouble of putting poison in her polish bottle, then calling Lucy Ellen to come back.

"Thanks." I picked the file up. "How did Darnell take it?"

"He's devastated. He's beating himself up for going to the woods because she begged him to go to that wedding. You know how grieving people are. Playing that 'what if' game, trying to change the time they spent with their loved ones the twenty-four hours before death." Max made a great point. Everyone always second guessed themselves when it came to a loved one's death.

"He didn't know she was an organ donor and was real sad she couldn't give life after death."

"That's a shame." I wondered if she'd been able to give her organs if she would've been remembered for that kindness instead of the mean-spirited bad reviews she'd written.

"He wondered if he'd been there whether he could've stopped someone from killing her, but I'm not sure if he couldn't have stopped her from getting her nails done." He sighed.

"I'm not sure anyone was going to stop her yesterday from getting her nails done." It made me wonder if Lucy Ellen had just pushed Tina to her limit after I'd left. Maybe Tina told her to come on in and get her nails done, poisoning her in the process.

Even though Tina had said she didn't see or talk to Lucy Ellen after Lucy Ellen left. Was she covering up what she'd done?

"I'm not sure she had them done so much as did them herself." He picked up his camera from the desk and turned it on. It took a minute for him to scroll through the photos. "Here, this is the right hand. Scroll across five more times to see the photos of all five fingers."

Each photo showed a finger and nail. I wasn't sure what he was pointing out.

"I can tell you don't paint your nails often." He got up and stood over me. He pointed out, "Lucy Ellen Lowell was right-handed." He took the camera from me and showed me another photo. "This is her left hand. They are pretty perfectly polished from her using her right hand."

"She painted her own nails because her left hand painted her right nails and the nail polish is all over her fingers," Poppa chimed in. "Good observation, Max."

I repeated what Poppa had said.

"Exactly. The poison got into her skin. Her toes are pretty perfect, but there's some on the skin around her toes too." Max showed me more Perfectly Posh colored photos.

"Then Tina didn't kill her directly," Poppa observed.

"Tina could still have given her the nail polish with intent for Lucy Ellen to paint her nails with the poisoned polish." The possible scenarios rolled around in my head.

"Tina might say that she didn't kill Lucy Ellen and she didn't know the polish was poisoned. So we need to find the cyanide." Poppa was good at trying to put himself in the mind of the killers.

"Possibly." I nodded.

"Kenni." Max looked over his shoulder. Poppa looked at Max, but Max didn't see Poppa. "Who are you talking to?"

"Myself. Can you give me a sample of the nail polish?" I asked. "I'd like to take it to my lab and have Tom Geary analyze it for the compound. I'd like to know exactly what ingredients she uses. Tina makes her own polish. If this is the polish she makes, it makes even more evidence against her."

"I can do that if you sign it off as evidence in the investigation." He put the camera back on the desk and walked out of the office. "I'll email you the photos."

It didn't take him but a second to snip off Lucy's fingernail into a baggie that I could take to Tom Geary, the owner of the lab I used located in Clay's Ferry, the next town to Cottonwood.

"Here you go." He held it out. "Let me write it in your file and mine, give me a signature, and you're out of here."

"Sounds good," I said and took a nice long look at the fingernail while he got the paperwork completed.

After a few quick strokes of my John Hancock on the papers, I had my evidence and was back out to the Jeep where Poppa was waiting.

"What are you thinking?" he asked.

I turned the engine over and looked around and made sure no one was around to see me talking to myself.

"What you said about it being a premeditated murder is right. I'm not sure Tina has that in her, though anger brings out the worst in people." I looked out over the wheel and put my hand on the gearshift and put it in drive.

"She might if I was right that she didn't technically paint Lucy's nails herself. The evidence is the evidence." He looked down at the baggie in the seat. "Tom Geary is our guy to find out. And where is the bottle of fingernail polish?"

"I don't know." The Wagoneer rattled out of town onto the country road that led to Clay's Ferry. "Tina looked in the back of her shop while I nosed around up front."

"Did she really look in the back or did she get rid of the evidence?" Poppa and I loved to play the back-and-forth what-if game that came along with solving crimes.

"We can look to see if there is a dumpster behind her building, or even search her house." That was a good thought. "Search her house," I said again and nodded.

The late afternoon sun was starting to go down. Daylight savings time really did make the days feel so much shorter with less sun. If I was going to get to the lab before it closed, I better hurry.

I grabbed my phone and called Finn.

"Don't tell me you're cancelling" was how he answered the

phone.

"No." I couldn't stop my smile. Poppa grumbled. "I called because Max gave me the report. The poison was put in Lucy's fingernail polish. Max also gave me a fingernail clipping so I can take it to the lab for Tom Geary to analyze. I have to see if this is Tina's homemade polish, because if it is, I'm afraid I'm going to have to haul her in."

"Oh man. This is big." Finn wasn't joking. This was huge. "Right here before the wedding too."

"What does that mean?" I asked.

"When the mayor found out about this being a homicide, he came to Darnell's house while I was securing it. He asked if we could not focus on the investigation so much since it overshadowed his wedding." He paused and I took the moment to speak up.

"Are you kidding me?" I gripped the wheel and pushed the pedal down to go faster. "He's such a jerk. I'm not doing it. I'm going to get to the bottom of this with or without his approval."

Chance Ryland and I had a rocky past. He wasn't a big fan of mine and it was no secret he didn't vote for me. But we could all see who the sheriff was now. I didn't get there by kissing his fanny either.

It was hard to get too upset thinking about Mayor Ryland's arrogance as I drove this stretch of country road. It was easy to get lost in the pops of fall colors and trees that lined the curvy road. The last bit of sun forced its rays through the branches and made little light dots on the pavement.

"He knew you'd say that." Finn laughed. "I told him you were the sheriff and he needed to take it up with you."

"Yeah, I'll take care of him." I was so tired of him and secretly wished someone would run against him, but like me, he was running unopposed this election.

Another four years of him as our mayor was going to be the best lesson in patience. Then I'd also have to deal with Polly Parker and her new title of being his wife. The mayor's wife. I laughed out loud thinking about her wearing a sash around town with a crown on her head. Something I wouldn't put past her.

"What are you laughing at?" Finn asked.

"Nothing." I shook it off. "But I will say that it's strange that the mayor would want us to actually keep the investigation on the down-low or even stop it until after the wedding."

"I said that same thing to him," Finn said. I loved how he and I thought alike on most instances when it came to cases. "He said that he didn't want anything to overshadow the wedding. He even said something so cold."

"What?" I asked, worry in my head. What if the mayor knew more about Lucy's murder than he wanted to give up? He was a member of the Hunt Club. It was full of the good ole boy mentality and Mayor Ryland definitely had that attitude.

"He said that no matter how quickly we solved it, Lucy Ellen was dead now and would still be dead after the wedding." As Finn said these words, I could actually hear them in Mayor Ryland's voice.

It made me shiver.

"I'm about to turn into the lab. I'll be over after I grab Duke from the department and go home to change." I had to focus on the task at hand and deal with Mayor Ryland later.

"I got Duke a little bit ago. You won't make it by the time Betty leaves and I didn't want to leave him there alone." His kindness made me love him even more. "I'll stop by your house and grab him some food and your clothes if you want."

"That's a plan. I've got a pair of sweatpants on my dresser with a t-shirt. And grab my sweatshirt off the chair." I knew I should probably try to dress in something like jeans and not sweats, but I wanted Finn to love me for me and not my attire. "I'll see you soon."

"Kenni, be prepared to take Jolee's call. She's not happy. I'll tell you about it when you come over." We said our goodbyes and hung up.

"Anything new?" Poppa asked.

"No. I was going to have him look in the dumpster behind Tiny Tina's but decided to wait to see what Tom has to say about the nail polish." There I went again, procrastinating on the investigation when I knew in my gut the polish was going to turn out to be the weapon like Max had concluded.

"You're making sure you're doing it right." Poppa was so good at getting the clues and the evidence before I flew off the handle and went around arresting anyone. "We have to make sure because remember, you're only an election away from being without a job."

I gulped. He was right. There was no job security in being an elected official. I loved my job so it was worth the stress.

The lab was on the edge of Clay's Ferry. It was a small brown brick building. The bell over the door signaled my arrival.

Tom Geary walked into the waiting room where I stood with the baggie. His grey hair was a little thinner since the last time I'd seen him.

"Sheriff, to what do I owe the pleasure?" Tom outstretched his hand and I shook it.

"Pleasure?" I asked. "Even though I do enjoy seeing you, I wish it was under different circumstances."

"I'm assuming what you want me to look at is in that bag?" He looked at the baggie in my hand and nodded.

"It's a fingernail." I held it out for him to take from me. "My victim has been killed by cyanide and it's believed the polish painted on her nails was tainted with it."

"That's awful." His brows furrowed. "Your Poppa and I did a lot of cases with poison put in drinks, but this is a first."

Poppa beamed with pride. He loved being around Tom. They worked a lot of cases together and that's why I still used him. There weren't any labs in Cottonwood and I didn't have time to send it off to the state-run labs, so I continued to have clearance to use Tom's lab when I needed quick results. This was one of those times.

"I remember some of those. Poppa really enjoyed your friendship." I wanted him to know how appreciative we were.

"I was about to go home, but I'll get right on this." He continued to look at the nail.

"I also wanted to know if you could give me a breakdown of the polish. One of my suspects owns a nail salon and she makes her own polish. I just so happened to be there when the owner of the salon said some bad things about the deceased, who was at the time living." It was a lot to take in. Something none of us would even think up, but a cold-blooded killer would. "The deceased even asked for this particular polish and the owner refused to give it to her."

"I see." Tom's lips pressed together in a thin line. His nose flared. "With all my years of working with the police, I shouldn't be surprised by a lot of the outcomes, but this." He shook the baggie. "Sorta sick."

"Thanks, Tom." It was time for me to get back to Cottonwood and put this day behind me.

Once we got back into the Jeep, Poppa was quiet. He stared out the window deep in thought.

"Tell me what's going on up there." The days were getting darker earlier as the seasons started to melt together. It took a lot to stay motivated after sunset when the cold set in. Heading home to Finn keeps me going and staying focused.

"The whole fingernail-polish thing is crazy. Not only does it say that someone is sick, but who would do that to a woman?" he asked. "Another woman." He answered his own question.

"That's what makes Tina look like the killer. She knows about making polish, she makes that particular color, and she did threaten Lucy Ellen." I just felt awful about it. "Why on earth would Tina do something like that? Because of some no-show appointments? Bad reviews? Why would she kill her?"

Sure, when I was there to ask her if she'd seen Lucy Ellen the night before Lucy's death, there were a couple of clients who'd cancelled.

"Was it the reviews that spurred Tina to kill Lucy?"

Poppa's chest heaved up and down as a loud sigh left his body. "What about the other women in the shop when Tina said that? Who was there?"

"There was me, Jolee, and the bridal party, as well as Tina and Cheree." I still wanted to talk to Cheree just to make sure she hadn't talked to Lucy Ellen after she left the shop. "I need to expand my suspect list and go to the library to check out all the reviews Lucy Ellen wrote."

"It's hard to look at our friends and think they can do something so horrific." He had a way of giving me instructions without actually giving them.

"Yes. You're right. I need to go see and talk to everyone who was there that day. Apparently, Jolee isn't happy, and I plan on talking to Cheree tomorrow." I mumbled, "Then there's the Euchre bridal shower tomorrow night where I can feel out Polly and her crew."

"Time and patience will reveal all the clues we need," Poppa agreed. "Keep your eyes and ears open. All them gossiping hens will give you bits and bites of information that you can chew on.

Remember, solving a crime is putting a puzzle together. We have the pieces, we just need to fit them together."

Chapter Nine

"She wasn't happy." Finn's eyes stared at me. The gold flicker of the candle between us put a sparkle in his eyes. Or maybe it was the look of a satisfied belly from all the pizza we'd just consumed.

Duke lay on the floor underneath the table and Cosmo was curled up in my lap. Finn wasn't a big cat person, so when he took in Cosmo I was completely surprised. Not me. I loved all animals, and Cosmo was a great cat.

No matter how much he told me that my best friend, Jolee Fischer, was mad that I'd sent him to ask her questions about her argument with Lucy Ellen Lowell, I couldn't really raise a care because the way he looked at me overcame any feelings I had about anything going on in my life at this moment. Not even Poppa keeping a close eye on us between his wisps in and out of Finn's house bothered me.

"If she's not guilty, she has no reason to be mad." I shrugged and took a nice long drink of the red wine Finn had grabbed from the Dixon's Foodtown wine aisle, which wasn't much different from Boone's Farm Strawberry wine.

"I think she was more mad that you didn't question her, kinda like girl talk or something." He wiped his mouth and put his napkin on his plate.

He stood up and walked over to his phone that was connected via Bluetooth to his speakers and put on a slow romantic tune. Jokingly, he waltzed over and stuck his hand out. Immediately I put Cosmo on the floor and took Finn's hand. He pulled me up and swept me into his arms.

There were no ballroom dance moves or fancy footwork; it was simply swaying back and forth in the middle of his kitchen until we eventually scooted into the new addition.

"You know you make living here so much easier." His voice was low and seductive as he whispered into my ear.

My hands were snug around his waist. When I looked up, I noticed his calm and steady gaze.

"I am going to use my vacation time during Christmas to go back and visit my parents." Finn's voice was a velvet murmur in my ears.

Finn was from Chicago, where his parents and sister still lived. They were a close family. I'd only met his sister once when he first moved here. She'd come to visit and was actually going to take Cosmo, but fairly quickly found out that she was allergic.

"Christmas?" I asked, trying not to sound like some whiny girl, but I loved Christmas. If there was anyone I wanted to spend it with, it was Finn.

"If we plan now, we can get someone from the state reserve to come for the week and you can go with me." His gaze moved around my face like a soft caress. "I think it's time you met my folks."

"Are you sure?" I stopped the sway. "This is a big step."

Finn had once told me that he never took girls to meet his parents because his mother would hound him about them. I also remembered him saying that if he did take a girl home, it meant that she was probably the one. This sent my spirit soaring.

"There's no one I'd rather spend my Christmas with than all

the people I love and want to spend the rest of my life with." He raised his hand and slowly ran the back of his fingers down my cheek.

My chin dipped. He used the pad of his finger to tip my chin back up to look into those eyes that made my toes curl. I quivered at the tender touch of his kiss and knew that calling the state reserve was a priority in the morning. Though Christmas was a few months away, I knew I had to make sure it was a go.

It took everything I had to drag myself two doors down when it was time to go home and get some sleep.

Solving Lucy's murder should've been the main thing on my mind as I tried to go to bed, but it wasn't. My mind exploded with images of a happy Christmas spent in Chicago with Finn and his family, which caused me to lose sleep.

"Sweetly sang the donkey at the break of day!"

That couldn't be the voice of my mama singing to me at six a.m., I thought the next morning. "If you do not hear him this is what he'll say. Heehaw, heehaw, heehaw, heehaw."

The romantic night before with Finn still had my heart in a pitter-patter. I pushed Duke's head off the pillow next to mine and dragged it over my head.

"Sic her, Duke," I instructed my bloodhound. "Right in the jugular."

Mama continued, "You obviously hadn't heard the donkey." She cackled.

"Mama, no one in this room thinks you are funny at six in the morning," I mumbled under the pillow and pressed it tighter to my head as I wished her away.

"Get up. You have one hour until you have to be at the office and you're spending it with me," she proclaimed, swinging my closet door open.

"Remind me to take her spare key away." I reached out

from underneath the pillow and ran my hand down Duke's back. I tugged the pillow off my head.

Duke groaned, giving in to her. With both front legs out in front of him, he slipped them off the bed. He stood with his front paws planted on the ground and his butt on the bed, his hind legs dangling off the edge. He and I both watched as Mama went through my closet, pulling out clothes she wanted me to wear for the hour with her.

"I'm going to be spending time with you tonight at Euchre," I said, hoping it was enough together time to suit her.

"This morning, I thought we'd go for breakfast." She pulled out a floral-printed dress and held it out for me to see. "A healthy breakfast since you need to get off a little of that weight."

"If you think I'm fat now, wait until I get back from spending Christmas with Finn's family. I'm going to be explosive," I joked, knowing that it would send her into the looney bin that I wasn't going to be in Cottonwood on December twenty-fifth.

"You're what?" Mama gave me the eye. "Now you quit being ugly and teasing your mama." She held up another dress for me to put on.

I shook my head. Her lips twitched, her nose curled. She stuck it back in the closet and came out with a pair of brown sheriff pants and a long-sleeved uniform shirt. A much better choice, especially since I had to go to work after she lectured me on fitting into that darned dress.

I nodded. She snarled.

"Now get up and get ready." She threw the clothes on the bed. "Come on, Duke. Granny will take you out."

Duke didn't hesitate at the word "out."

"Mama, where are we going?" I asked and dragged myself

out of bed and into the bathroom to get my shower. I was going to need a long hot one to get me started on the right foot if I was going anywhere with Mama.

We only had two real breakfast spots to eat at in our small Kentucky town: Ben's Diner and On The Run food truck.

"Paula Parker's house," she hollered down the hall from the kitchen.

"Mama!" I yelled and ripped the shower curtain open. I wrapped my hair in a towel and grabbed my robe, throwing it on my soaking wet body. "What is this? Some kind of intervention? I've already agreed to counseling with Preacher Bing." I walked into the living room.

"For goodness sakes, I know you two are dating, but go get some clothes on." Mama held her hand to her chest like I'd just committed a sin.

Finn stood behind her with a cup of coffee in each hand and the biggest grin on his face. Now that was a face I'd love to see every morning. His smile was infectious and I returned it.

"Good morning." He looked so handsome in his brown sheriff deputy's uniform. "I wanted you to start your day off with a good cup of coffee from Ben's, but I hear your mom is going to take you out for breakfast."

"Thank you." I took the coffee. My body shivered as our fingers touched. He bent down and kissed me. Not nearly like last night, but I didn't care.

"Young love." Mama swooned. "To be your age again." She let out a happy sigh. "Finn," Mama batted her lashes at my beau, "my daughter is really trying to get my goat at this hour of the morning. Isn't she terrible?"

Mama gave me a slight shove toward the hallway. I padded back down to get ready.

"I'm wearing my uniform," I called over my shoulder.

"How awful of her," I heard Finn respond, and then I heard the sound of kibble being poured into Duke's bowl. "What on earth has she done?"

"She's saying that she's going to Chicago for Christmas and I know that's not true. I mean," Mama had on her dramatic Southern voice, "I know that Kenni'd never leave her mama alone on Christmas since she's my only daughter. Could you imagine the pain your mama would feel if you were her only child and she had to wake up on a holiday like Christmas alone?"

I stood with the front of my robe gripped in my hand next to my chest and the water dripping down the sides of my face with my ear up against the crack in my bedroom door. This was a test on just how well Finn could stand up to Mama. A test that I've always feared but never thought would come this soon, or this early, in the morning.

"Please be on your game," I whispered.

"Viv, I did ask Kenni to go to Chicago for Christmas to meet my family. It's only fair that my parents get to enjoy the presence of the fine young woman that you've raised. I want to show her off."

Finn was saying all the right things, if it were any other time of the year that he wanted me to meet his family.

"That just won't do." Mama's sweet Southern voice turned into a sweet Southern strict voice. One I knew all too well. "Your mama is just gonna have to meet her in January. Because we have the big Christmas festival here in Cottonwood and the annual parties of our friends. Kenni will be expected to be in attendance for all of them."

Shortly after she gave Finn a good tongue lashing, I heard the backdoor slam.

"Honey?" Finn called. "I don't think your mama is taking

you to breakfast anymore."

About that time my phone chirped a text. I walked over to my bedside table and looked down. It was Mama. She said she'd see me at the Parkers' residence in ten minutes. Too bad Finn didn't make her madder.

Chapter Ten

I would've texted Mama back and told her twenty minutes because I wanted to get in a little smooch time with Finn before he headed back to the office, but if I did that she'd have been fit to be tied.

Duke went to the office with Finn and twenty minutes later, Poppa and I pulled up in front of the Parkers' gated mansion. Their massive house wasn't far off the road and it was rumored they'd built it that way on purpose. To show off. It was just like Pete and Paula Parker to do such a thing.

I pushed the button on the intercom and was greeted by one of their hired staff through the black box.

"Kenni Lowry here for breakfast." I looked over at Poppa and rolled my eyes.

They knew I was coming. Why didn't they just leave the gate open?

When the gate did open, I pulled the Wagoneer up and around their circular driveway and parked it right in front of the large lake in the middle of the drive. The four concrete swans as big as my Wagoneer were already spitting water out of their beaks.

There was a woman at the front door with a tray in her hand and she seemed to be awaiting my arrival. On the tray was a green glass of yucky-looking something or another. There was a piece of paper propped up in front of it that read my name.

"I'm assuming this is for me?" My brows rose.

The lady nodded. I could tell she was trying not to smile after I took it off the tray and dumped it over into the Parkers' bushes next to the front porch.

"That was tasty." I smiled and put the glass back on the tray.

I walked into the house. "Sheriff." Paula Parker acted as if she'd not seen me in years. Her nose curled up like it always did and her face squished up like a prune.

I gave her the once-over, noticing her chin-length brown hair looked like she'd just gotten it done by Tina. Her signature pearls were clasped around her neck. I couldn't help but wonder what time the woman had gotten up to get all dolled up for little ole me.

"I don't think this involves me." Poppa fidgeted nervously after he ghosted in and ghosted right back out. "I'll go do some digging around about Lucy. I'll meet you at the Lowell house," he said, reminding me that seeing the crime scene was my number one priority this morning.

I instantly wanted to protest because now I was really alone here and suddenly uncomfortable.

"It's so good to see you this morning, but I can only stay a minute. Duty calls." I tapped the utility belt around my waist with my gun nestled in the holster. "Not to mention I've got an appointment with Preacher Bing."

"Yes. I'm delighted you and Polly are getting along so well." Paula's head tilted to the side, a fake grin on her face. "That's what we wanted to talk to you about, dear." She swung the door open.

In the foyer stood Mama, Polly, Pete Parker, and Mayor

Ryland. I glanced back over my shoulder and didn't see anyone else's cars. This was an ambush.

"Won't you come in?" Pete Parker stepped up and gestured toward the fancy parlor room where only the good company was entertained.

"Only if you got something better to drink than that green stuff." I smiled.

"I'm so sorry. She's not a morning person." Mama made all sorts of excuses for what she'd call bad behavior. "Ain't that right, Kendrick."

My ears perked at the sound of my full name as a red alert that Mama wasn't pleased with me.

"You get in here and behave." She jerked me to her like they couldn't see. "You hear me?"

"Are you joking me?" I whispered back as she led me into the room along with everyone else.

Her eyes widened, her lips squeezed together. She was as serious as a witch in a broom factory.

"We won't take up too much of your time." Mayor Chance Ryland raked a few of his fingers through his slicked back salt-and-pepper hair.

Sweet, sweet Polly with her perfectly coiffed blonde hair, black slacks, and white cardigan with her own set of pearls locked around her neck had her hands clasped in front of her, the big diamond ring sparkling as she stood next to her man.

"It's been brought to my and Polly's attention that you are investigating the murder of Lucy Ellen Lowell. As you know, since we did pick you as our maid of honor, we feel like your time for the next couple of days is best spent on making sure Polly's needs are met." His words brought up an anger in me that boiled my insides.

"After all, it's an honor to be maid of honor, especially in the soon-to-be first lady of Cottonwood's wedding." Paula did all the talking for her daughter as Polly stood there with a big (fake) smile on her face. "We don't mind if Deputy Vincent does all the investigative work. It'd be different if you weren't in the wedding. But duties are duties and right now Polly is your duty."

"This is all dandy and good." I took a step back. "But do you hear yourselves?" I looked at each one of them square in the eyes. "You're asking me to give up the safety of all the citizens of Cottonwood for a wedding?"

And I thought I was here to learn how to keep from eating the next couple of days so I wouldn't ruin any wedding photos with my happy fat.

"This is ridiculous." I shook my finger at the mayor. "If this little meeting was to get out to the public, I think everyone would be rather upset with our mayor. Don't you? In fact, didn't you tell Deputy Vincent that you'd like for him to take over the investigation because..." I hesitated for more of an effect and I tapped my finger to my temple. "If I recall correctly, your exact words were, and I quote, 'no matter how quickly we solved it, Lucy Ellen was dead now and would still be dead after the wedding.'"

"Umm." Mayor Ryland shifted side to side.

"I understand that you want to keep everyone in the Hunt Club on your side since you are a member and when election time comes, they do have a lot of influence in Cottonwood. But to use and abuse the power the citizens of Cottonwood have entrusted in you to stop an investigation where there's a murderer on the loose? And all you care about is that your wedding goes off without a hitch?" I didn't have to say much more than that.

The silence that hung in the air was as thick as the spring fog after a midnight storm.

"As mayor I'm not asking anything of you. As Polly's future husband, I'd like to see my bride get everything she'd like." His chin lifted as he sucked in a deep breath through his nose and looked all high-brow down at me. "Of course I don't want a killer on the loose and the citizens are my number one priority."

"Well, technically," Polly laughed, "I'm your number one priority."

I watched with amusement as Mayor Ryland hushed her by waving his hand.

"I thought we were here to talk about the wedding dress?" Mama stepped up. "Not talk about my daughter's job that we elected her to. To honor, protect, and serve. Or how we elected you to run our town."

I looked at Mama. She looked at me.

"I'll be darned." I smiled. "You do have my back."

"Damn right I do. This is a disgrace to not only my daughter's hard work, but to the citizens of our small town, and we are leaving." Mama grabbed me yet again, dragging me out of the room like she dragged me in a few minutes ago.

"Don't worry!" I called out before I slammed the front door behind me. I yelled extra loud so they could hear me. "I'll be at the wedding on time. See y'all then."

Mama stood by the Jeep.

"I'm sorry about that in there. I swear Paula told me that we were going to discuss that gawd-awful dress." She tried to keep a straight face. "It was ugly. And you aren't fat. You are perfect the way you are."

"Thanks, Mama." I hugged her. "But Finn does make me happy. And going to see his family at Christmas is just a week. You get me and him all year long." I pulled back because I wanted to see her face. "I love you and Daddy so much, but I'm going to Chicago with Finn. I'd like to have your blessing, but if you can't give it, I'm sorry."

"No." Mama shook her head. "It's fine. When your daddy and I had only you, we'd actually talked about the possibility of sharing you on the holidays with another family. Talking about it and the real action are completely two different things." She looked away and her eyes shifted back to me. She looked down her nose. "Only this one time though. Next year you're home for Christmas."

"Promise." I made the criss-cross with my finger over my heart and gave her another last hug. "I've got to get over to the church and meet with Polly and Preacher." I rolled my eyes.

"Alrighty. I'll see you tonight at Euchre." She gave me another hug and a peck on the cheek before she and I went our separate ways.

As soon as I got back into the Wagoneer I checked my phone for any messages in hopes Tom Geary had left one. Nothing. I was surprised I hadn't heard from him last night about the polish.

The Cottonwood First Baptist Church was on the south end of town and I took my time driving through town, going in and out of streets to get there. There was no way I wanted to get there before Polly.

The church stood off the road with about an acre between Main Street and the building itself. There was a large staircase that led up to a huge concrete covered porch with five large pillars holding it up. Four large doors were evenly built along the porch that opened up into the vestibule of the church. Preacher Bing stood next to the far-right door greeting the people before service and the far-left door saying goodbye after the service.

Today he was eagerly waiting in his office with Tibbie Bell, the wedding planner, and Polly Parker in the basement of the church.

"I'm sorry." I looked at my watch. "I'm not late, am I?"

"No." Preacher Bing gestured for me to sit down.

His hair was plastered to his head and his bangs hung down on his forehead. He was tall and lanky. He looked like Lurch from the The Addams Family and he always scared me. Today was no different.

"I thought I'd talk to Polly first," Preacher Bing said.

"We were just discussing how you and Polly became friends." Tibbie's brows rose. "Isn't that right, Polly?"

Polly nodded. Her perfect bob swung back and forth, her horse teeth glistened.

"And the big falling out we just had at my parents' house." Polly couldn't just leave well enough alone.

"We didn't have a falling out." I preferred to call it something else. "We had a disagreement because your future husband would like me to turn the other way about Lucy's murder until after your wedding."

"Is that right, Polly?" Preacher Bing turned to Polly.

"Well...um...I..." It was like she'd been caught out in public without makeup on and everyone saw her.

"Don't worry." I knew she'd be all upset if the man of God was disappointed in her. "I'd never compromise the office and Mayor Ryland didn't either after we discussed it. Right, Polly?"

I secretly prayed that I wouldn't be struck dead by lightning from lying and saving Polly's face while in church.

"Right." Polly nodded and the stress fell from her face.

"Fine. We can move on. Now, Kenni, what is your recollection of the first time you met Polly?" Preacher Bing folded his long lean fingers—they had always creeped me out—and tilted his head to the right as if he were really interested.

"Well, we both grew up here so I don't remember the first

time I met her." I scooted up on the edge of the chair, hoping it'd be a little more comfortable. "I remember she always had the best of everything. But she's younger than me."

"But he wants to know any fond memories." Tibbie was reaching deep and she knew it.

"When I was on a stakeout a year or so ago, I remember seeing her and the Mayor kissing, proving the rumors true."

"Kenni," Polly gasped.

"I'm sure she meant it was innocent." Tibbie patted Polly's delicate little hand and narrowed her eyes at me as she tried to cover up what I really meant.

"Actually, it was only a rumor at the time, but I was trying to check out Polly's alibi since she was accused of killing poor old Doc Walton." My lips pressed together as I thought of the memory. "Here we are today." I clapped my hands together. "All happy now."

Preacher cleared his throat.

"Do you and Polly have any memories of going to the movies, a fun girls' weekend?" Preacher sat back in his chair.

"No." I shook my head. "Polly had her own set of friends."

Tibbie adjusted herself in her seat in an aggravated sort of way.

"What about the time at bible school when she befriended Toots?" Poppa appeared and came to my rescue.

"I do remember vacation bible school and how sweet it was when she gave Toots Buford her cookies."

The tension melted from the three of them as their shoulders dropped and smiles formed on all of their faces.

"Tell us about that," Preacher encouraged me.

"As you know, Polly was always in the younger group. Toots was new and she definitely didn't come from the same background as Polly. Toots didn't have on the cute matching clothes that included the shoes and a bow in her hair like Polly. Toots seemed really hungry because I remember her gobbling up that cookie and small cup of Kool-Aid they gave us." It was actually a very sad memory. "I remember Toots was sitting by herself and Polly went over there and sat right down next to her at the picnic table."

In some sort of way, I was trying to get Polly to see that I wasn't the right choice and she should ask Toots to be her maid of honor.

"So her kind heart attracted you to become friends with her." Preacher looked happy and satisfied with my answer. "Polly, I think you've picked a maid of honor who truly knows your heart and kindness."

"You mean I'm here because Polly was questioning me taking part?" I give a sideways look to Tibbie. "Because I was under the distinct impression that we were both going to get some sort of counseling."

"Thank you so much for your time, Preacher." Tibbie hopped up and nodded before she rushed us out of there.

"Oh, Kenni." Polly grabbed me into a hug when we stepped out into the hallway. "You are so wonderful for remembering that. I'm so excited to hear your toast talking about my kind and giving heart."

"We need to head on over to the florist." Tibbie lightly touched Polly's elbow.

I snarled at Tibbie. Polly gave me the two-finger wave before giving me the call-you-later gesture.

Next week's wedding couldn't come soon enough. Being in Polly Parker's wedding was proving to be a full-time job. I had to put all that in the back of my head and do my real job. On the way over to the Lowell house, I mentally went over the evidence we had and tried to think of anything that didn't point to Tina.

The polish, the argument, and the negative review on the salon all pointed directly to Tina. There had to be something I was missing.

Duke was on the front porch as if Finn had put him there to be a guard dog. He and Darnell were in a face off.

"Hey, Darnell." I looked between the two as *The Good, the Bad, and the Ugly* theme song played in my head. "Duke." I patted my leg with my free hand while my other one gripped my bag. "What's going on here?"

Darnell ran his hands through his hair.

"Darnedest thing." He pointed to my trusty sidekick. "I came by to grab some more unders," apparently his word for underwear, "and I couldn't get past this deputy." He snickered a little.

"Duke takes his job very seriously. Says crime scene. Do not enter." I gave a quick head nod. "Come on. I'll let you get your drawers."

Duke had changed his tune when I showed up. He'd always been such a good dog. He'd even taken a bullet for me and the city gave him a medal for it. I swear he knew it because ever since then he'd been even more protective.

"Finn?" I called out once we stepped inside. It was eerie going into the house since the other night. The last time I was here, it was a routine call where we thought Lucy Ellen had died of a heart attack. Well, not me, since Poppa had showed up, but to the rest of the world.

Now it was definitely a crime scene, making it an altogether different feel.

"If I didn't think it wasn't fittin', I'd just have you go get them for me." Darrell was hesitant to go into the house. "I just don't know what I'm going to do. We didn't have no young'uns or nothing. No family left." His voice trailed off and his eye focused on the spot where he'd found Lucy.

"I know people have been saying it a lot, but you have a lot of friends in the Hunt Club and every one of Lucy's friends." I tried to offer as much of a condolence as I could.

"What's his story?" Poppa appeared and stood in the exact spot of Lucy's body outline. "Where was he again?"

"I know that we talked a little bit about your whereabouts, but do you mind if we talk for a second after you get some clothes?" I asked Darnell.

"Sure, Sheriff." He nodded toward the hall. "Can I grab my stuff now?"

About that time, Finn came into the room.

"Sure. Say, Finn." I smiled, remembering last night and how amazing he was. "Do you mind going back to Darnell's bedroom with him and letting him get some clothes? I want to make sure he doesn't disturb anything, just in case."

"Yes, ma'am." His eyes shifted to Darnell. "Ready, sir?"

Darnell simply nodded and headed on back with Finn, leaving Poppa and me standing there.

"You know he was in the woods." I looked at Poppa.

"Yes, but the husband is always the prime suspect." Poppa had always checked out the next of kin or family members when he investigated a crime. "All t's crossed and i's dotted." Poppa winked.

"I plan on stopping by the gun show too." Thinking about the little show the mayor had put on this morning started to get my blood boiling again. "I want to see how the women reacted to Lucy's death and if there was any tension between them."

While Poppa and I talked, I looked underneath the couch to see if the fingernail polish was there. It was my number one priority to find the polish Lucy Ellen was wearing on her nails.

With no luck, I walked outside to Darnell and Finn. Darnell

had gotten his unders.

"Can we talk now?" I asked Darnell. He agreed. "Exactly where were you again the night of Lucy's death?" I didn't want to say murder.

"In the woods with the guys to get our cabins and stands ready. We also have our annual gun show going on, but the wives really like to stay there and take care of it." His eyes were so dark and hollow. He'd really aged in the last twenty-four hours. Grief did that to a person. "Don't take this wrong." He put his hand out in front of him as if it were going to ease the tone of his words. "Most women don't understand guns. They like to take part in the gun show, but as a rule, we like to keep two members of the Hunt Club at the gun show if the others are out hunting so questions can be answered. The women take the money and process the necessary paperwork for a sale."

"Can you tell me who you talked to and everything you did from the time you last saw Lucy Ellen until you found her?"

"Didn't I tell you all this already?" he asked.

"You did, but you've had a day to process what's happened. Research has found that after a period of time, things will start to come back to you that you didn't remember while your body was in a state of shock. You might remember the slightest of things that you think are minor, but in an investigation it could be that one little link we are looking for to help connect evidence." I stopped to make sure he understood me. "So why don't you tell me the last time you saw Lucy Ellen face to face?"

"That morning I was getting my gear ready. My bag packed, food she'd made for me to take. I got my rifles ready. She said something about getting her hair done for the wedding and asked me again." He stopped. His voice cracked. "She begged me to be home for the wedding and I told her no." He buried his head in his hands, overcome with grief.

I reached over and rubbed his back for a little comfort.

"I'm sorry." His lips pushed together, his face squished up. "I just don't know what I'm gonna do."

"One day at a time." I patted and rubbed. "Go on and tell me about what you did after you pulled out of the driveway," I encouraged him.

"Drat." Poppa stomped. "Some kids are in the Dixon's Foodtown about to steal something. I can't have you leaving this interrogation. I've got to go scare them off before Toots Buford calls Betty at dispatch."

I took a deep inhale and let out the big breath to clear my head from Poppa talking to me.

"I'm sorry. I'm just trying to figure out what Lucy's last actions were and it helps if I know where you were and what was going on. If she was upset and all that. Go on," I said again.

"Like I said, I told her I couldn't go to the wedding." He shuffled his feet. "I regret it now. All the men were going to go hunting wild hogs and I had to go. I just couldn't think of them bringing home a hammy and not me. Now I wished I'd just said yes to her. Finn said something about poisoning. What on earth? Do you think maybe she got into something and wasn't murdered?" He teared up again. "The thought of someone wanting my sweet Lucy Ellen dead is beyond me."

I did a little more rubbing and patting. He clearly wasn't ready to talk.

"I don't know. But before I let you go, you did say something about Lucy Ellen complaining about Tina Bower's salon, Tiny Tina's." I wanted to hear it one more time.

"Yeah. She and Tina have this love-hate thing. Tina cuts Lucy's hair too short on purpose, Lucy Ellen claims. Then she got the foot fungus thing and blamed that on Tina. But then they go eat lunch and all that." He sighed. "Women. I just don't understand them. Why? Do you think Tina did this?"

"I don't know. I'm just eliminating everyone at the moment." I wasn't going to show any cards to him. With his arsenal of guns and in his grief, I wasn't sure what Darnell would do when we found out who killed his wife.

"I'm staying out at The Tattered Cover Books and Inn if you need anything else." He gripped the plastic bag. "Please keep me posted."

"I will. I'll definitely be calling with more questions." It was only fair to let him know to expect me to call him. After another day or so, I was sure he'd remember more. "Before I let you go." I paused. "Did you know she was an organ donor?"

"She talked about it, and it was just like her to always give to others." He painted her as a saint.

"What are you thinking?" Finn asked after we heard Darnell's truck door slam and drive off.

"I'm thinking we have to find that bottle of nail polish. I also want Tom Geary to call me with the results of Lucy's fingernail and I certainly am thinking about that ugly dress I have to wear in front of the entire town on Saturday." I laughed.

Finn took me in his arms.

"We'll get to the bottom of this. I'm sorry I've not found anything to help in the investigation. It's like the killer has vanished." He gave me a hug. "I'm going to head on over to Tina's house and see if she'll let me look around. What I find over there will help us decide who we look at next."

"Sounds good." I gave him a kiss through the window of the Jeep after I got in to drive away. "I'm going to stop by the library."

We said our goodbyes and I called Betty at dispatch over the walkie-talkies to see if anything from Dixon's was called in.

"Not a thing going on. Just a lot of calls from the gals about

Lucy Ellen and what we're going to do about bell choir at Christmas." She ho-hummed. "You don't want to do bell choir, do you?"

"Betty, I don't know. Let me get through this investigation first, then I'll worry about months from now." Why was it that everyone started to worry about Christmas months in advance?

Even stores were already selling wrapping paper and ornaments.

"Finn's gone to Tina's house to talk to her and I'm going to head on over to the library." I gave Betty the schedule so she'd know where we were in case a call did come in and she'd be able to determine who could get where faster—not that Cottonwood was that big, but I prided myself on the efficiency of a two-officer department.

"Don't eat out for lunch. Your mama brought you a salad and she told me to make sure it was the only thing you eat." Betty snickered on the other end. "Happy fat" was the last thing she said before she clicked off the walkie-talkie.

Suddenly I had a hankering for one of those big pastries and a hot cup of coffee the library offered to their patrons.

Chapter Eleven

The old white colonial house that was centuries old and stood next to the courthouse had been converted to the Cottonwood Library before I could remember. I'd spent many hours getting lost in different fictitious towns as a child while Mama enjoyed her many group meetings there.

The rush of wind pushed past me when I opened the front door. The smell of paper and old books wrapped around me in a welcoming and comforting hug to my soul. It was such a distinct smell. The kind that immediately brought back those fond memories.

I waved at Marcy Carver, the librarian, when Duke and I walked past the reference desk. She smiled and continued to talk on the phone that was pinned between her ear and shoulder as she typed on the computer keyboard.

The library only had three public rooms. The children's section was probably the most popular, then there was the fiction section that held all of the various genres, and the non-fiction room, which was where I was going to check out the last few weeks of the *Cottonwood Chronicle*. It'd have been much easier to look up the *Chronicle* online, if only they put them online as they were published. Unfortunately, Marcy was still in the old-school era and was so very far behind in getting the most recent papers on the internet. Once she told me it was Malina Woody's job since she was the assistant librarian. I'd even gone as far as bringing it up at one of the town-council meetings that Edna Easterly, the owner of the *Chronicle* and editor-in-chief, should have the equipment to upload the paper, but that failed miserably.

The non-fiction room had a few tables with computers as well as a card catalog for the periodicals. It was also the area where the library had the sweets and coffee bar.

Today was an assortment of cupcakes that definitely didn't come from Dixon's Foodtown. These were fancy. The heavenly smell even made Duke stick his nose up in the air and dance around.

"You can't have any of these." I eyeballed the chocolate on chocolate right off. There was a business card from the Sweet Shop. I took one and put it in the front pocket of my shirt. "This one is perfect."

With a couple pumps of the coffee carafe in a paper cup and the cupcake, I walked over to the card catalog, setting my goodies on top of it.

In order for me to get the back issues, I'd have to write down the exact dates I wanted. I drew my finger down the little drawers and pulled the one with the letter C. The little filing tabs clicked along the top of the drawer as it slid to full extension.

I decided on the last two months' issues. This way I could look up Page Two and see exactly what Lucy Ellen had reviewed. Two months would seem like a long enough period for someone to fester over her words as well as see any potential loss to their business.

There was a basket of scrap paper and tiny pencils, like the ones you'd see at mini-golf, in another basket. I grabbed one of each and wrote down the information from the card catalog.

The squeaky wheels of the book cart screeched from behind me. I turned around when it stopped. Malina was running her finger from one hand down the spines of a row of books and had a book in the other hand.

"Hey, Malina." I held the pieces of paper and noticed her hair was cut shorter. "Where is the Sweet Shop?"

She tucked a piece of her hair behind her ear. She'd gone from long brown hair to a more stylish asymmetrical bob and even added highlights.

"It's a new shop in the strip mall next to Hart's Insurance. They have the neatest desserts." Her smile reached her eyes. "You picked a good one."

"Yeah. It looks so good." I didn't care that I needed to fit into that maid of honor dress. I was going to eat that cupcake for brain power. At least thinking that made me feel better. "I see you're still keeping the new hairdo. It looks good." I smiled.

"Thank you, Kenni." She raked the tips of her fingers down the bob. She bent down and patted Duke a couple of times behind his ear.

"Are you still getting it cut at Tiny Tina's?" I asked.

"There's no one else in town." She stood back up, shrugged, and picked up another book off the cart. With the end of the spine, she shoved a space for it on the shelf.

"How's the Tattered Cover?" I asked about the hotel where Darnell Lowell was staying. Malina worked the front desk there part-time.

"It's all good. I'll be picking up more hours during the fall and holiday season, but it's a little slow right now."

Tourists loved to come to Cottonwood during the holiday season since it was on the antique registry. The Christmas Festival also brought in a lot of visitors. Our small town was beautifully decorated, almost dipped in Christmas.

"You said that you still get your hair done at Tiny Tina's. Did you ever see Lucy Ellen Lowell in there?" It might be a long shot, but I thought I'd give it a try.

"Ummm..." She sighed, twisted her lips, and rolled her eyes to the sky. "No," her head shook slowly, "I don't think I ever saw her in there. But I did see your mama in there once or twice getting a pedicure from Cheree. She's just the sweetest. Your mama, that is."

"Isn't she though." I spared Malina the truth about my mama and her role in me being in Polly's wedding. "Anyway," I held the pieces of paper out to her, "can you grab these issues of the *Cottonwood Chronicle* for me?"

She thumbed through them. "What are you looking for?"

"I'm going to look up all the editorial reviews and comments, along with anything I can pull up about Lucy Ellen Lowell. I know she did a lot of reviews in the paper and it seems like a good place to start to see what people knew about her or who had a tiff with her." I usually wouldn't say so much to Malina, but she was in the public with gossip fluttering around.

"Marcy might know a thing or two." Malina couldn't hide the devious smile on her face. She leaned in and looked up under her brow to see if anyone was around before she said, "Marcy secretly hates—hated—Lucy. Lucy Ellen came in here to use the computer to do her reviews after someone would make her mad. Marcy told her that she was mean and she wasn't going to let her do it anymore. Lucy Ellen told Marcy that she paid taxes and she could use whatever computer she wanted and Marcy couldn't stop her."

"Really?" I never figured I'd put Marcy Carver on a list of persons of interest for murder, but she was definitely going on there for me to talk to.

"It didn't stop Lucy. She marched right on over to that

computer." Malina pointed. "Lucy Ellen wasn't smart enough to erase the history off the computer and while she was here, Marcy turned off the internet. When she left Marcy went over to the computer to see what Lucy Ellen had written. Lucy Ellen didn't write a review for the store she'd intended to when she came in. She wrote a bad review about Marcy and how she didn't let people use their tax dollars to use all the library has to offer." Malina laughed. "I've never seen Marcy so mad in her life. She erased the history and the review before she turned the internet back on." She shrugged. "We've learned that if we turn off the internet, Lucy Ellen's review is lost."

"Did Lucy Ellen ever come back in?" I asked.

"Oh, yeah. Only when I was working though." Malina shrugged. "I don't care about other people's business."

Sure you don't, I thought.

"It's a free country and Marcy was right." Malina shook her head. "Lucy Ellen got what she had coming to her."

"Marcy said that? It seems a little harsh to wish death on a few silly reviews," I noted as Malina nodded with pursed lips.

"You'll have to ask her about that." She turned and glanced towards Marcy's office door that was closed. "Anyways, I've got all these issues of the *Chronicle* on the computer already." She handed the papers back. "I've been trying to get them uploaded the day the paper comes out. Edna is paying me extra to get them up on the new website."

"New website?" I asked.

"Yeah. Edna said there's a big market with online subscription services, which just sends Marcy over the edge." Malina laughed.

"Why is Marcy upset?" I asked.

"Because she says the internet is going to shut down the library and we'll all be out of a job. That's why she doesn't want anything to go online as quickly as I can do it." She leaned around me and looked. She leaned back and whispered, "Between me and you, I'm going to go work for Edna and her online subscriptions. I'm going to be giving my two weeks right before the Parker wedding because Edna wants me to cover and write a story on it since I'm invited."

"Congratulations. I didn't know you wanted to work at a newspaper." I clearly remembered Malina's nose always being stuck in a book.

"I want to be a writer like Beryle Stone." She smiled fondly as she spoke about the only famous (now deceased) citizen of Cottonwood, who was a bestselling author. "Look out, literary world." She brushed her hands in front of her like she was brushing away anything that might get in her way. "Here comes Malina."

"Good luck." I crumpled the papers in my fist and threw them in the wastebasket on my way over to the computer. The cart squeaked out of the non-fiction room with Malina pushing it.

I wondered how Marcy was going to take Malina leaving. It sounded to me like there was some tension between the two librarians' ideas. It was none of my business and I didn't have time to even think about it.

Duke laid down next to the computer table I sat down at to look up the back issues of the paper.

After I logged into the computer, I surfed the web for the *Cottonwood Chronicle* website. It popped up. In the search box on the left sidebar, I typed in the dates for the last couple months. The articles appeared on the screen with another box overlapping it asking for my subscription information. There were two ways I could do this: I could either get Malina or Marcy to get me the paper copy, or I could easily subscribe through the sheriff's department and have any sort of access I needed from work or home.

I opted for the subscription, which was smart on Edna's part. With the sheriff's credit card information all typed in and my password set, I was in business and flipping the online paper to Page Two, the social page.

There wasn't anything interesting or from Lucy Ellen in the first couple of papers that I looked through, but there was a review in the third paper about six weeks before today's date.

Lucy Ellen had written a review about Pet Patch and in particular shaming Faith Dunaway, the owner, for not carrying a certain cat food. For a minute, I tried to remember if the Lowells had a cat because I hadn't seen one. Regardless, the article said Faith refused to order any in and that she wasn't a very good business owner because she didn't cater to the needs of the citizens of Cottonwood. She also went on to say that Faith wasn't a good citizen of Cottonwood because she didn't believe in hunting and protested many of the Hunt Club's events. There was even a picture of Faith where she'd gone to last year's gun show and threw fake blood on none other than Lucy Ellen Lowell. Edna had gotten a really good shot. Underneath that photo was another one of Faith cleaning out cages at the local SPCA with a snarl on her face. I wasn't sure what it was about, but I was about to find out.

The rest of the papers had the reviews I'd already known about. The one with On the Run food truck and the latest one on Tiny Tina's Salon.

"How are you this morning, Sheriff?" Marcy called on my way past the reference desk.

"Good. I see the children's theater is going well." There was a puppet show going on in the children's room.

"Oh, the kids love it. We're starting to work on the

Christmas puppet show for the Christmas benefit. They asked us to join them. I think it's a wonderful idea since parents will open their wallets up to just about anything that supports their children." She clasped her hands in front of her.

"You're getting a jump on things. We haven't even had fall yet." If I didn't know better, I'd think Cottonwood citizens wanted to skip fall and head straight to winter. Not me. I loved fall in Cottonwood.

"It's just around the corner and will be here before you know it. What brings you here?" she asked.

"I needed to look through some of your back issues of the *Cottonwood Chronicle* for a little work." Without even telling her what the work was, I knew she already knew.

"I'm assuming you're here to look up the reviews Lucy Ellen Lowell's always done and narrowing down suspects?" she questioned.

"We are looking at all possibilities, yes." I rocked on the heels of my shoes.

"Let me get those for you." She gestured to the room behind the reference desk where they kept the paper copies.

"Malina was very helpful in telling me how they're online now. So I jumped on your computer and even made me an online subscription." As I spoke to her, her neck got red and it crept right on up to cover her entire face.

She cocked a brow. "Is that so?" Her question was followed by a deep inhale and her glare turned toward Malina, who just so happened to be walking by with a fresh load of books to reshelve.

"She mentioned that Lucy Ellen Lowell came in here to do her reviews of shops and her opinions about the people who own them." I said. When I didn't get an immediate response, I asked, "what did you think about that?"

"What? Lucy Ellen's reviews?" She leaned her hip on the edge of the desk. "I thought they were mean spirited if you want to know the truth. When I saw her coming through those doors, I would watch her. She'd sit at one of these desks and gnaw on her bottom lip as she typed away. She'd stop and look up like she was really thinkin'. Then she'd start typing again. Like in a mad rush or something. I know this probably isn't right, but I'd pretend to be re-shelving some books behind her to see exactly what she was doing. If she was writing something that looked like a review to the *Chronicle*, I'd hurry to my office and turn off the internet."

"Why would you do that?" I asked.

"Because she was mean. Her reviews were only in the *Chronicle* to hurt people." Marcy looked down at her fingers. "I know it ain't fittin' to say, but if you asked me, she got what she had coming to her."

"Did she ever write a review about the library?" I asked.

Marcy smiled. "About that," her brow rose, "she complained about the internet and I told her that the form was saved and would send to the *Chronicle* anyways, though I knew it wouldn't. She didn't know better. Last time I caught her doing a review and turned off the internet, she said she was going to write a review about the internet service because she really did believe it was the bad internet here that turned off and not me."

"Some of her reviews obviously got through. How did that happen?" I asked since she said she'd kept a close eye on Lucy Ellen.

"I'm not here twenty-four seven." She let out an exhausted sigh. She slid her gaze over to Malina. "Some people don't care about other's feelings." She returned her stare at me with a blank look on her face.

"You didn't happen to have any ill words with Lucy Ellen,

did you?" I asked.

"For heaven's sake, no." She shook her head. "I wasn't about to get in a piss and vinegar fight with her over some reviews or how I felt like she was nasty to people when she didn't get her way. It was best to stay clear of her." She looked back at Malina. "Malina, a word with you."

"Sure." Malina walked over.

"In my office." She jerked her head to the side. "Sheriff, it was good to see you. Bye, Duke." She didn't give me time to say goodbye. She quickly turned on the balls of her feet and stomped back to the office.

As I walked, I thought about the articles. I'd completely forgotten about the call from last year's gun show event. When I went out to see Faith about it, she claimed it was free speech. I'd given her a ticket for disorderly conduct but what had transpired from there, I wasn't sure. But I was about to find out.

"You want to get a treat?" I asked Duke when we got back into the Wagoneer.

He jumped around, panting and wagging his tail.

Pet Patch was the cutest pet store with grooming services. Faith took great care in making sure all animals were welcome there. She didn't sell animals, but she did give out names to reputable breeders of all sorts of different animals. She was the go-to gal for pets in Cottonwood. Duke loved it there. He just didn't like the seasonal baths I brought him in for.

The front door mooed when I opened it, making me giggle. The doorbell wasn't the regular ding; Faith had special ordered one that sounded exactly like a cow.

"Duke!" Faith made it a point to always greet the animals when they walked into her store.

He ran over, knowing exactly what was waiting for him in her pinched fingers.

"I see you brought your mama with you," Faith joked like she always did. She patted Duke as she gave him the treat. "Kenni, I hear you're going to be in the big wedding."

Faith had shoulder-length strawberry blonde hair and sparkling blue eyes. Definitely not the look of a killer. *Good cover up though*, I thought as I greeted her with a friendly smile.

"I love that bird apron," I said.

She ran her hands down the front of it and they ended up in the front pockets where she took out another treat.

"Can he?" It was nice that she asked before she just did it like the rest of the citizens.

"Absolutely." How could I deny the cute dancing hound?

"We have a special on Duke's food this week plus a manufacturer's coupon." She walked in the direction of the dog food. "It's really a great deal."

"I didn't come here for some, but we can always use a good deal." I followed behind Duke who was close on Faith's heels. "Actually, I came to ask you about your relationship with Lucy Ellen Lowell. I'm sure you've heard she was murdered, and it's my understanding you were a little upset, as you should be, about the mean-spirited review she posted in the *Chronicle*."

"Mean-spirited?" Faith curled up on her tiptoes and reached up for the bag. I helped get it down. "I think it was downright hateful. I'm sorry she's dead, but it doesn't take away the fact that she was a spoiled brat. What she wanted and didn't get, she made a mess of."

"I went to the library and looked up the review. It said she was mad that you didn't carry a certain cat food. I didn't even know she had a cat." I hoisted the big bag of kibble up on my hip.

"She doesn't. She buys cheap cat food for the shelter. Sometimes I put food on sale right before the expiration date. It started piling up once and I knew she did some volunteer work there. I won't because it's a kill shelter and I can't donate to that. Don't judge me." Faith was aware of how that sounded.

"I'm not judging." Though it was strange that she didn't want to donate food to keep them living instead of the other fate. Still, I was there to gather information, not judge her.

"Lucy Ellen came in and we made an agreement that I'd call her when food was about to expire." It sounded like a good collaboration. But where did it go wrong, I wondered as she continued to talk. "The food I was giving her expired so quickly, I decided not to carry that manufacturer anymore because I was losing money here at my shop. So I discontinued it. A month or so later Lucy Ellen came in. I told her about the food and how I didn't have anything at this particular time."

Faith stopped and gulped.

"She had the nerve to tell me that I was the one killing the cats at the shelter by not giving the food to them at a discount and that was blood on my hands. She ranted on how I didn't really care about animal rights and it was only a ploy for me to get people to come into the shop." Her voice cracked. "Her words are still painful to this day."

"Did it hurt your business?" The malicious words could've played a big part in a motive for Faith to commit murder, but losing money and altering her lifestyle was an even bigger motive.

"That's the funny thing. Business started booming. People were coming in here saying how they knew I was a reputable store because they knew she'd write those nasty reviews out of hate." She coughed up a laugh. "I called her and actually thanked her for the review."

"I bet that didn't go well." My jaw tensed.

"She hung up on me." She rolled her eyes. "Like I said, I

hate that she died, but whoever did it was someone who she probably wronged one too many times."

We made our way up to the front of the store where the registers were located.

"Can you tell me where you were the night of her murder?" I asked. Her mouth dropped, her eyes widened. "Just doing this with all the people who got a bad review from her."

"I was actually in Atlanta at the big pet expo. I've got plane tickets, hotel stubs, and even my husband who was with me along with hundreds of other shop owners who can corroborate." She had an alibi and if I did need to look into it I would, but nothing told me she was lying. "Bloomie and I have to keep our grooming licenses up because they expire every year. So while I was there, I did that all over again because I'm almost expired."

"Thanks for being up front and honest." I started to reach for my extra money in my pocket.

"Don't worry about it." She shooed my hand away. "This bag is on me. Does he know?"

"About his appointment on Saturday?" I asked. "No," I mouthed.

She threw her head back and laughed. The alarm over the front door mooed, signaling the arrival of Duke's most favorite dog groomer and Faith's partner, Bloomie Fischer.

"Duke." She bent down and put her arms out. He darted toward her and slid into her lap with his arms and paws extended forward; tail wagging and kisses ensued.

"I can't wait to play with him Saturday," Bloomie whispered over his shoulder.

"We've got to go." I patted my leg. Duke enjoyed one last good scratch from Bloomie. "Alright, Casanova, let's go. See y'all Saturday."

Duke and I walked out very happy customers of Pet Patch. He had a few more treats and I had a free bag of dog food.

Though Faith had some good information on why she and Lucy Ellen had words, it still didn't give me any more information on who killed Lucy.

Going back to the salon to talk to Cheree was my next stop. I checked my phone to see if by chance I'd missed a call from Tom Geary. Nothing. I put my phone on vibrate and put it in my back pocket.

"It's awful about Lucy Ellen Lowell," Cheree whined when she saw me walk in. In one swoop, she pulled her long red hair back and up into a perfect top-knot. "And to think we just saw her."

"We sure did." I looked around. For the late afternoon, I found it odd that there weren't any customers in the joint.

"Who on earth would ever want to hurt her?" she asked in a sweet Southern drawl. She reached into her purse and took out her glasses, nestling those on top of her head too.

"I was hoping you could answer that." I couldn't stop myself from looking at the nail polish bottles in hope the Perfectly Posh would show up.

"What on earth do you mean?" Cheree stopped what she was doing and stared doe-eyed at me.

"I don't come here a lot, but I couldn't help but overhear all the gossip that took place after Lucy Ellen left here."

Cheree looked at me as if she didn't know what I was talking about.

"Oh, come on." Sarcasm dripped from my lips at her ignorance. Was she hiding something? "When Lucy Ellen left here, there was a lot of talk about her and everyone's dislike of her," I said, as if she needed reminding.

"That?" She pish-poshed. "That's all it was. Talk."

I hummed. "Talk? Innocent talk and then she shows up dead?" I shook the bottle of fingernail polish to help mix up the top oily layer with the rest of the polish.

"Lucy Ellen was wearing a color on her nails that looked pretty similar, if not the same as Perfectly Posh," I said, stopping Cheree dead in her tracks. "Cheree?" It wasn't the exact reaction I'd expected, but at least it was something. "Cheree, are you okay?"

My phone vibrated in my pocket. I slipped it out to look and see if it was Tom. When Toots's name popped up, I hit the off button, sending her to voicemail.

"Kenni," Cheree gasped, causing the freckles on her face to widen a smidgen. "That night around eight, I got a call from Art Baskin about our security alarm going off." She tapped the rose gold watch on her wrist. "I'd left here around seven thirty and drove straight to Cowboy's Catfish to get my to-go order. After Bartleby gave me my food, I came back here and that was around eight fifteen-ish."

Art Baskin was the owner of the only security-system provider in town.

"You know it only takes a couple of minutes to get here from there. When I showed up at the shop, Art was waiting in his car. We came in to check it out and there was nothing wrong in here. I turned the alarm off. Art asked if I wanted to call the sheriff, but I said no. I called Tina and told her that I came by and no one was here. I asked her if she wanted me to call you and she said there was no reason to. You know them heathen kids nowadays like to come in and color their hair all sorts of crazy colors. I figured they were trying to steal some color. Nothing looked out of place, but Tina did say the next day that her Perfectly Posh was missing. The last person we saw with it was Lucy Ellen Lowell." Cheree recalled how Lucy Ellen wanted to buy it.

"You didn't see or talk to Lucy Ellen after she left here that afternoon?" I asked.

"Why no, I did not." She said as if I shouldn't ask such a thing, "What are you insinuating?"

"I'm only trying to figure out what Lucy's actions were after she left here. You and I both heard and saw how everyone reacted when she was here." There was no sense in not being up front and honest with her. "You didn't make a police report about the break-in?" I asked.

"Nope." She walked around and plugged in all the styling tools they used on their hair customers. "I didn't see the need to call anyone because there was nothing missing. We have two of everything that is worth anything." She walked around and pointed. "Two hair dryers, two flat-irons, two curling irons, all the nail things, our work stations. If something like a small bottle of nail polish or even hair dye was missing, we'd never really know. I use nail polish and all the hair products when Tina isn't here, like she does when I'm not here. We don't keep records when we finish with a product."

My phone vibrated. I pulled it out.

"Excuse me. I need to take this." It was Tom Geary. "Hello, Tom."

"Sheriff, I'm sorry I couldn't get back with you sooner. I just wanted to make sure and do a little research before I gave you the findings." He was so thorough and I liked that about his lab. "Do you have a second?"

I walked out of Tiny Tina's and got into the Wagoneer so I could grab my notepad and write down what he was telling me.

"I do. Let me grab my pen and paper." I shut the door once I got in.

"I'll be faxing over the report to your office," he informed me. "In the meantime, I felt like I should call you and tell you the results myself."

"That's great." I dragged my bag across the seat of the Jeep and opened it, taking out my pen and paper. "Okay, tell me what you found out."

"The polish base is a clear topcoat that can be broken down into ethyl acetate, butyl acetate, and alcohol." He said words that I had no idea how to spell correctly so I phonetically did the best I could until I could get the report. "It was the color that made me do the longer test that took all night. The color was actually derived from eyeshadow. There was also a lethal dose of cyanide in the small bit of nail that I tested."

"What is your conclusion?" I asked.

"I actually narrowed down the compounds of the eyeshadow to MAC Pink Venus eyeshadow. With the level of cyanide in there if someone had painted even one nail with the lethal polish, they would've died, much less all of her fingernails and toes." It was all I needed to hear in order to march back into Tiny Tina's to see exactly how Tina Bowers made her polish.

"If you wouldn't mind getting that report over to the office ASAP, I'd be eternally grateful." My eyes slid across the seat.

Poppa appeared and stared at me with a dropped jaw and opened eyes.

"Did you say MAC as in the boy's name?" he asked in a whisper.

I nodded.

"I'm faxing it as we speak." Tom said, and I hung up.

"There's a bunch of makeup in the back room of Tiny Tina's that's got the name MAC on them in big bold letters." Poppa looked past my shoulder and out the Jeep window toward Tiny Tina's.

"Looks like we have the ingredients, a motive, and the

killer." I gnawed on my lip. I punched the button on the side of the walkie talkie. "Betty?"

"Hey, Kenni," Betty answered as if I were calling to see how she was doing, not as though this was business.

"I need you to get Judge to get me a warrant to search and collect some evidence at Tiny Tina's. I need you to fax it over to the salon. You'll find their fax number over in the Rolodex on my desk. And it needs to be ASAP. Tell Judge that I'm here now and I've got a big lead." I left out the part that the big lead was Poppa's ghost telling me that in the back room was the same makeup brand that Tom Geary had said was one of the main ingredients in the weapon used to kill Lucy.

"Gotcha." Betty clicked off.

Out of the corner of my eye, I saw Tina's old Corolla pull up and her getting out of the car. She tossed her cigarette butt on the pavement and twisted the toe of her shoe in it. With a heavy sigh, I got out of the car.

"Tina," I called before she entered the building.

"Hey, Kenni. Are you ready for your big nail day?" She smiled and used the tips of her fingers to add some volume to her brown hair.

My heart broke in tiny pieces because I knew that smile would falter pretty quickly after we started talking.

"I guess, but that's not why I'm here." I gestured for us to go inside when someone pulled into the parking lot. "Can we go into the back where you make your nail polish? I think you called it the color room the other day."

I thought I'd ask instead of waiting on the warrant.

"Sure." She looked at me with her brown eyes. The smile was gone. She stuck her purse behind the counter. She said to Cheree, "I'm going to talk to Kenni for a minute. I'll be right back."

That was easier than I imagined, I thought when she readily agreed to me going back there.

"That's fine. We had a bunch of cancellations today." Cheree nodded at the door. "I've got one manicure and that's it."

"Great," Tina moaned.

As I looked at Cheree, many questions popped into my head. Before I went to the back room, I just had to know.

"Cheree, you didn't make a police report?" I asked again to make sure I'd heard her correctly before I took Tom's phone call.

"No, I didn't. You can ask Art." She shrugged.

"I will, but in the meantime, why didn't you make a report?" I asked.

"There didn't seem to be anything taken or out of place. Just a break-in, so I didn't see the point in going through the trouble of calling you to make a report. You are a busy woman."

"I appreciate that, but I'm also the law and I take pride in my job." I pointed to the desk. "Do you mind making me a copy of the client lists for the past couple of weeks?"

"Sure." She hurried over to the desk and grabbed the appointment book. "I'll get to it right now." She flung the printer that sat on the front desk next to the phone open and smacked the appointment book on it.

I walked into the back room. It was just a storage room with a steel table in the middle. Tina was standing near the table where she mixed the fingernail polish, but Poppa stood by the makeup on a different table.

"Right here." Poppa pointed to the makeup. "This one is Pink Venus."

I swallowed hard and walked over to Poppa's table, careful not to touch it. I needed to treat this as a crime scene where the weapon was made.

"So you use a clear fingernail polish and add eyeshadow to it to make your signature colors?" I asked. "Where were you between eight p.m. Tuesday night and four a.m. Wednesday morning?"

Tina's head shot up.

"First you send Deputy Vincent to my house, where he found nothing." She glared. "And now you come to my job and question it. What is it that you want from me, Kenni? Are you saying you think I harmed or killed Lucy Ellen Lowell?"

"I want the truth. Simply answer my questions." I rested my hand on my holster. "Do you use this MAC Pink Venus to make your Perfectly Posh nail polish?"

One question at a time.

"Yes." There was a bit of defensiveness in her voice.

"I'm going to go out on a limb and say that you're probably the only person that Lucy Ellen Lowell came to for her manicures. And it just so happens that the day before her murder she came in here and you actually said that maybe you should've cut her hair and had the scissors slip."

"You've got to be joking me." She was getting fidgety and hostile. "It was gossip. That's what we do here. Oh." She twirled around. "I forgot. You don't come to these sort of places. You don't gossip. You're the sheriff."

I detected a hint of sarcasm in her voice.

"I can name five other people here that day that also had a beef with Lucy." She held her hand up in the air and uncurled a finger with each name. "Me, Cheree, Polly, Jolee, and Faith Dunaway."

"Tina, Lucy Ellen Lowell was murdered." I watched her actions.

"It wasn't by my scissors." Her leg jutted out to the side, her hip followed as she planted her hands on her hips. "You can't be back here." She flung her hands in the air just as the ringing phone followed up by the beeping of the fax machine echoed in the air.

"I think you're going to find that the fax coming through is a warrant to not only search the salon but also collect evidence that proves the murder weapon used was Perfectly Posh nail polish laced with cyanide poisoning." I took a deep breath before I gave the final blow. "Perfectly Posh made with MAC Pink Venus eyeshadow."

"You are seriously accusing me of killing Lucy?" she asked.

"Where were you between eight p.m. to four a.m.?" I asked again out of curiosity because the truth was that the polish could've been poisoned at any time of the day, but just in case I could tie her to the scene, it'd make it a lot more solid.

"I..." She gulped. "I'm not going to answer that. Isn't there a fifth amendment, or is it first? Either way, I'm not answering."

"Ummm...Kenni." Poppa caught my attention. I followed where his eyes were focused. "I think we've got some cyanide."

There was a bottle sitting on the ground. There were no markings on it, but I took Poppa's word for it.

"What are you looking at?" Tina asked.

"What is in the bottle, Tina?" I asked and walked over to it.

"I have no idea. Maybe some sort of chemical." She shrugged, nodded, and harrumphed all at the same time.

"Tina Bowers," I unhooked the cuffs from my utility belt, "you have the right to remain silent. I'm arresting you for the murder of Lucy Ellen Lowell." I continued to read her the Miranda Rights. She interrupted.

"Kenni Lowry, you've lost your marbles." The piss and vinegar started to pour out of her mouth. The cuffs clicked as each tooth on the lock clicked tighter around her wrists. "This beats all I ever seen. Cheree! Cheree, get in here!" She screamed at the top of her lungs.

"What's wrong?" Cheree ran in with a look of fright. There were papers in her hand. She handed them to me.

"That's wrong. Where did that come from?" Tina pointed.

I gave Cheree a chance to look over the poisonous bottle of substance labeled Cyanide.

"Cyanide?" Suddenly it appeared as if she had a quick and disturbing thought. "Tina, you didn't…"

"I ought to smack you silly. Hell no, I didn't." Tina put up a stronger guard now. "Did you? Did you put it here?"

"She could've." Poppa let out an anxious cough. "I mean…"

Before Poppa could say it, Tina finished it, "You've got a beef with her too. It's not just me. After all, you're the one who said we needed to not let her make appointments anymore."

"It was you that said you'd like her dead." Cheree came unglued. "You're the one who complains about her day in and day out. You're the one who does her nails. I never use your homemade fingernail polish. You know I go down to the dollar store and get fifty-cent nail polish. You're the one being the freaky mad scientist."

"Look." Tina pointed at me. "She's trying to turn us against each other. We won't let you pin this on us. We didn't do anything to Lucy Ellen Lowell no matter if we can't tell you how that bottle got there."

"Where were you the night of the murder?" I asked Tina again.

She drew her shoulders back and stuck her chin up in the air. When she curled her lips together and pinched them so tight that the edges turned white, I knew I had my answer. She wasn't going to tell me come hell or high water what she'd been doing when Lucy Ellen was killed and I had no other option.

"Anything you say can and will be used…" I tried to

continue the arrest policy when I unfortunately had to use some force. "Tina Bowers, straighten up right this minute," I jerked her wrists closer together as she tried to pull them apart.

Both of us stopped jerking the other. Her hands stopped flailing and there we were, in a stand-off. Only I knew I was going to win.

"Don't make me parade you through the front of the salon acting all nutso. I'm more than happy to take you out the back door," I suggested.

"I've done nothing wrong. I'm going to be using my one phone call now, thank you." Her chin tilted to the side, her eyes drawing down her nose on me.

"You can use the phone once we get to department." I shook my head and pointed to the door. "Go on."

She took in a deep breath, curled her shoulders back, and took the first step out through the beads covering the opening of the storage room.

"Lookie here, y'all." She held her cuffed hands way up over her head as she talked to her clients. "Kenni Lowry. Sheriff Kenni Lowry is crazier'n all get out. Arresting me for killing Lucy Ellen Lowell when I did no such thing."

"Let's go. Cheree, I'll be right back. I'm gonna have to ask all y'all to leave. The salon is shut down until further notice." I had to grab her by the arm and lead her out the door.

"You know what, Kenni," Tina spat. "This is all fine and dandy if I were a criminal. But I'm not and I can't wait for Wally Lamb to tear you a new one."

"Yep, me either." I opened the back of the Wagoneer and stuck her inside. I stood by the door and watched as three women filed out of the salon with half-done nails.

"There goes rent. Right on out the door. In a few minutes, you singlehandedly ran me out of business." Tina grunted and moaned. She leaned over to the rolled-down window. "Be sure to write in someone else's name on the election ballot. We can't have a nutso sheriff running around arresting people for no good reason!"

A low deep groan escaped me. "Tina, if you can prove your whereabouts and what you were doing at the time of the estimated death of Lucy, then I'm more than happy to let you go."

Cheree walked over and leaned against the car.

"Now what?" she asked.

"I'm going to go in there and take a few things for evidence and fingerprinting. Then, Betty Murphy will call you when we release the salon." It was standard procedure. "If you'll excuse me." I knew this wasn't the last time I was going to talk to Cheree, but I wanted to get Tina out of the environment that was making her nervous and hostile.

I still didn't have a clear-cut answer to where Cheree had been. Granted, she said she called Art Baskin and gotten food. Both of those would be easy enough to check out, but what about all the in-between?

I took a few steps away from the Jeep so I could talk to Betty at dispatch.

"Betty?" I called into the walkie-talkie.

"Go ahead, Sheriff." She was quick.

"Please get the cell ready. I'm bringing in Tina Bowers for more questioning on the murder of Lucy Ellen Lowell." I clicked off.

"Oh my stars." Betty gasped. "Oh my goodness gracious."

"Thanks, Betty." I clicked off again and pulled my cell from my back pocket. I scrolled down to find Finn's contact and hit the green call button.

In the meantime, Cheree was holding a cigarette for Tina to

puff on.

"Not in my Jeep!" I snapped my fingers at them, only to receive a glare from Tina.

"Any luck with Cheree?" Finn asked from the other end.

"It just so happens I'm bringing in Tina. Tom called with the report and it should be on the fax machine when we get there. He was able to break down the components of the polish to the exact make of the eyeshadow." I was trying to talk fast so I could hurry back in the Jeep and get to the department and beat the gossip.

"Eyeshadow? I thought it was fingernail polish." Finn was all sorts of confused.

"Meet me at the department and I'll explain all of it to you there. Oh, and I found a bottle of cyanide in the salon."

"I found it." Poppa poked his chest as if Finn could hear him.

"Anyway, I shut down the salon. We need to go through it with a fine-toothed comb. Tina Bowers won't give me a valid alibi. I had no choice." My voice drifted off because the thought of Tina being the killer was unfathomable to me.

But people killed for a lot less. And all the evidence pointing to her was found in her shop. To me that was as good a reason as any to make an arrest, though Wally Lamb might try to prove otherwise.

"He'll meet you there." Cheree had her cell up to her face and was talking to Tina.

"Tell him to bring me something to eat. I'm starving." Tina sat back and suddenly looked very comfortable in the back.

Cheree gave her a hug through the window and walked away. I waited until Cheree was gone before I made sure the Wagoneer's doors were locked and Tina was safe until I went back in and bagged the cyanide bottle, the MAC makeup, and a few of Cheree's bottles. If there were fingerprints on the cyanide bottle, I wanted to have Cheree's in case.

I got in the Jeep and started to pull out of the parking lot, but not without Tina giving me some lip.

"I garonteeeee," her Southern accent had a different take on the word, "you're gonna regret this."

"I hope I do," I muttered and turned toward downtown. "I really hope I do."

Chapter Twelve

"On what basis, Kenni?" Wally Lamb paced back and forth in front of the only cell we had in the department.

Tina was all sprawled out on the small cot eating a catfish special from Cowboy's out of the Styrofoam carryout container, not paying any attention to her lawyer or me.

"Wally, she won't tell me where she was on the night of the murder during the period Max has estimated as time of death. Not that she had to be there, because the murder weapon was the nail polish she made. The ingredients were broken down by Tom Geary's lab over in Clay's Ferry. The report is right here. All the ingredients, including the cyanide, were found in her salon."

After I'd brought Tina back to the department, I sent Finn over to the salon to see if I'd overlooked anything and clear the scene. He took more photos but didn't find anything else.

"Not to mention what she said after Lucy Ellen left her shop the other day in front of me." It was something I just couldn't forget.

Wally stopped and looked at Tina through the bars. He raised his hand and dragged it through his slicked-back blond hair. He let out a deep breath through a small opening in his lips. I couldn't tell if he was frustrated with me or with Tina. Regardless, his stress was showing on his face.

"There are no other suspects?" He finally turned around to me.

"I can't tell you everything. I can say that the evidence is piled against Tina." My eyes shifted between him and Tina.

Betty wasn't fooling anyone. She was acting like she was doing some filing work, but she had one eye on the cabinet and one eye on our conversation.

"Where is this polish that you claim to be the murder weapon?" he asked.

I cringed.

"I don't know." I bit the edge of my lip and prepared myself for his wrath.

"You mean to tell me that you accuse my client of making deadly fingernail polish after she had gossiped in her hair salon, because we know that there's no gossiping going on in a hair salon." He mocked me. "Then you think she polished the deceased's fingernails with it, but you can't find the actual polish to test, just the fingernail of the deceased?"

"The fingernail is really all we need to prove it was tainted. I'd like for your client to hand over the bottle so we can have a murder weapon. If she can provide that, I'm sure we can come up with some sort of deal with the prosecutor." I was laying all my cards out on the table. He and I both knew the fingernail was enough, but I knew the actual bottle the polish came from would help me seal the case.

"Besides, Tina was heard and seen making threats about Lucy," I reminded him.

"So did half the other people in the salon that day according to you and everyone else I interviewed. I also talked to Art Baskin and he said that the alarm would only go off if someone had broken in," he said flatly. "My client was set up and I'm going to prove it. She made a silly gesture. People make veiled threats all the time. It looks like to me that someone has set my client up. You've got the wrong person in custody and I demand you let her go this instant."

"Wally." I sucked in a deep breath. "I'm going to hold her for twenty-four hours."

"Twenty-four hours?" Tina jumped off the cot. "I've got to do your nails and the rest of Polly Parker's bridal party."

Just as if the floodgate opened up, the door of the department flung open.

"I demand you let Tina Bowers go into my custody," Mayor Ryland demanded with Polly Parker at his side.

"Yes!" Tina grasped the bars with her hands and shook them. "Demand it, Mayor."

The scene was spiraling out of control quickly.

"First off, Mayor, I appreciate you and Polly coming down, but this is an open investigation. So you are not welcome. Secondly, I'll let you know how the investigation is going when I'm done here." I wasn't about to let him take charge.

Finn walked in and nervously looked around. His hands were filled with evidence bags.

"Thank God you're here." Polly put her grubby little hands on Finn's arms and brushed down it.

It took everything in my body not to go all girl-crazy on her, but I knew I had to keep myself in check. I seemed to be the only sane one here. But I couldn't guarantee I'd stay that way if she kept putting her fingers on him.

"You've got to knock some sense into your girlfriend. Take control. Be a man," Polly pleaded with him.

"She's the boss. She's the sheriff. She knows what she's doing." Finn stepped away from her and went to his desk. He took out some evidence-processing forms while I continued to try to make order.

"Mayor, I've got this." Wally Lamb knew me and had worked with me many times. He knew that demanding things and trying to make me do something someone else wanted was not only a waste of time, but I'd do the complete opposite.

"But my nails." Polly wasn't budging. "We need Tina to do my bridal party's nails since Cheree can't do all of us."

"I'm sure you'll figure it out." Wally pushed them toward the door.

"Kenni Lowry, you are no longer my maid of honor! I want my dress back!" she hollered at me as the mayor took her out the door kicking and screaming.

I ignored her but walked out after them.

"Mayor, can I speak to you for a second?" I asked.

He looked between me and Polly. He whispered something in her ear. She stomped back toward me.

"I'm going to Cowboy's Catfish to get me a slice of pie." She snarled, her big horse teeth pressed together. Her lip twitched and she glared.

"That sounds so good." I couldn't help myself.

The mayor and I stood in silence until the door had closed fully.

"What is it, Sheriff?" He addressed me with an air about his title.

"It's not gone unnoticed that you're really trying to keep me from solving this case," I stated.

"That's not true," he retorted with his jaw tense.

"You do seem to have a vested interest in keeping me busy. Trying on dresses, doing manicures, seeing Preacher, hosting bridal events when you and I both know that Polly and I are far from being best friends," I stated the facts with a stern stare. "I'm only doing this as a favor to Tibbie and to get her business off the ground." The facts were the facts. "Where were you the night of Lucy's death? To be more specific, Tuesday night eight p.m. through Wednesday morning four a.m."

I felt like I needed to know exactly where he was, even though an alibi wasn't going to clear up who killed Lucy Ellen.

"You've got to be kidding me." He ran his fingers through his slicked back gray hair, loosing up a little of the gel that'd kept it in place.

"I don't joke about murder."

"What evidence would suggest that I have anything to do with Lucy Ellen Lowell's death? Why would I kill anyone, especially her?" His eyes clung to mine, studying my reaction.

"Well, you are a member of the hunt club, where it's been known that Lucy Ellen has caused a few problems. Not to mention she's a bit nosy, which Polly would hate. Then there's the fact that Polly really didn't want to invite Lucy Ellen to your big day. I can only think in fear she'd somehow ruin it. Then there's the election where you have to keep the good ole boys happy so they'll keep you in office and not turn on you right before the election. You wouldn't want to risk a write-in."

"Wednesday night, Polly and I were at a private cake tasting at the Sweet Shop for our wedding cakes. After that, we went to Luke Jones' basement to watch *Father of the Bride* with Polly's parents." His brows rose. "In honor of our wedding, Luke and Vita are playing *Father of the Bride* as well as *Seven Brides for Seven Brothers* because that happens to be Pete Parker's favorite movie."

"After the movies?" I asked.

He opened his mouth. His tongue played with the back of one of his teeth while his jaw jutted left and right.

"In honor of keeping my bride's reputation intact, I'm assuming you're going to keep this to yourself, but we've already moved into the cabin together." He sucked in a deep breath.

"Her parents aren't happy about it because they are old Southern and don't approve of us living together before we got married, so we've kept it very hush-hush."

You could've knocked me over with a feather. How on earth had the henny-hens not gotten wind of this bit of gossip?

"I went home and sent emails for work. You're more than welcome to seize my computer and check out what I was doing online after we'd gotten home. But I can assure you that I didn't kill Lucy Ellen Lowell." He straightened himself with dignity. "Now, if you'll excuse me, I need to get to my bride and you need to get back to Wally Lamb."

Even though Lucy Ellen was killed from the poisoning and Mayor Ryland could've added the poison before that night, I did recall Lucy Ellen saying to Polly that she was looking forward to talking to the mayor at the wedding since they'd not seen each other in months.

"Thank you for answering me honestly." I felt like we'd reached a level of respect that I'd never gotten from the mayor since I took office. "I'm sorry that Polly fired me as maid of honor."

He just nodded and both of us headed back into the department. Betty, Wally, Finn, and Tina watched as Mayor Ryland walked through the department and through the door that lead to Cowboy's Catfish. I turned to face them.

"This turned out good for you. That dress was ugly." Tina shrugged and eased back down on the cot.

Chapter Thirteen

Tina talked and talked and talked the entire rest of my time at the office. She just talked to hear herself. No wonder she was meant to own a beauty shop and spa. She had to be good at it. Mama always told me that Tina Bowers could talk to a wooden Indian.

By the time I'd gotten Duke dropped off at home and went to Euchre at Tibbie Bell's house, I was plum exhausted.

Tibbie lived on Second Street in a small house on the town branch. All the girls here for Euchre night were all gathered in the dining room where Tibbie set up tables for all the food that everyone brought. I'm talking delicious food too. These ladies took pride in their cooking. It was more like a repass, but no one was dead. I was happy too. I was in the mood for a good home-cooked meal of the semi-formal dinner style that featured collard greens and creamed corn paired with simple desserts like Betty Murphy's rice pudding.

"Kendrick Lowry."

My sudden urge for a big spoonful of the creamed corn went away with the image of an angry Toots Buford, who I could feel staring me down.

"I've called you several times. I left you many messages and you've never called me back." She looked like a puffed-up toad she was so mad. "It dills my pickle that you don't have the gall to call me back. To me, that means that you don't want to discuss the problem at hand."

"And what would that be?" I asked in a calm manner.

"You taking my rightful spot as Polly Parker's maid of honor, that's what." Her right leg flung out to the side and her right hand planted on her waist as she swung her right hip wide. "What do you have to say for yourself?"

"I'm sorry, Toots." I really wanted to tell her to take the job. I didn't want it. "I can't help who Polly picked to be in her wedding. I was just as surprised as you are."

"You are?" She reached around me and took one of the ginger snap cookies.

"Mmm-hmm," I ho-hummed. "If it's any consolation, she already fired me."

"I've been best friends with her since our days at the Toddler Inn preschool." Her brows knitted together. "I taught her how to do her hair and her makeup." She leaned in. "I even taught her how to line her lips so those big veneers of hers wouldn't overtake her wedding photos. And this is the thanks she gives me?"

That tip alone should've given her maid-of-honor status.

"Maybe she's going to call you now," I suggested with a hopeful voice. "I don't know what she's thinking. I'm just doing what Tibbie Bell tells me to do." I offered a sympathetic look.

"Well, I'm hurt to the core. She's pained me. I'm not even sure I'd be her maid of honor if she asked." She jabbed her long pointy fingernail in her own chest. "Painful I tell you." I nodded slowly.

I continued to nod, afraid to say too much in case it got back to Polly or Tibbie. The wrath of them was extra stress I didn't need.

After I filled my plate a couple of times and got the wonky eye from Mama, I headed into the room across from the food where Tibbie had set up the card tables for our Euchre night.

"At least you got to leave for a few minutes," Betty Murphy said about Tina Bowers's non-stop talking at the department.

Betty threw a card off suit, meaning she was out of trump. I didn't know if I would say she was being nice to fill in for Mama's Euchre partner who couldn't make it, or just wanted to come so she could be in on the gossip that was sure to circulate about Lucy Ellen and Tina tonight.

"She wouldn't shut up. Though she did have some really great decorating ideas." Betty offered a wry smile.

"How do you think Finn is doing with her?" I asked, scanning my cards for the right one to play off since Jolee had led off with trump and won the hand. I couldn't leave her there by herself in case she got ill or something, so Finn volunteered to stay the night at the department.

"He was at least nicer to me than you were to Tina, apparently." Jolee's eyes peered over the top of her cards.

"Jolee, are we actually going to even discuss this?" I asked with Mama and Betty looking at me. If there were anyone else other than the four of us at the table, I wouldn't have said anything.

"Excuse us." Jolee laid her cards face down on the table. "We need to go grab a brownie."

"Not Kenni," Mama chirped. "She's got a dress to fit into." She patted her belly. "Happy fat isn't happy in front of hundreds of eyes looking at you in the front of the church."

"Good thing I'm no longer in the wedding." It was with great pleasure I burst her bubble.

"What?" Mama cried out and pushed the chair back.

When she stood up to hurry after Jolee and me, the chair

fell backward and smacked on the floor. The other occupants of the four tables stopped and looked at us.

"I can't believe you'd think I'd kill someone. So when Finn showed up and questioned me, I nearly drove the truck into the telephone pole on the way to my next stop." Jolee was hurt. "Besides, I was with Ben all afternoon and all night."

Jolee and Ben Harrison were an item and they were always together.

"What do you mean you aren't in the wedding?" Mama squeezed herself between me and the brownies.

The questions both of them were throwing my way were just a jumble of words in my head. I reached around Mama and took a brownie and stuffed all of it in my mouth.

"Your daughter has ruined my career by arresting Tina. Polly Parker has the power to make me the most sought after wedding planner, but not now." Tibbie had to join in. "You could've arrested Tina after the nail appointments for the wedding."

"That's why Polly fired you as her maid of honor? The case?" Mama's brows furrowed. "The biggest wedding in Cottonwood. You're going to be known for this and it's not good. Couldn't you just take your time for once? It's not like Tina Bowers is going to run out of town or anything."

True, Tina probably wasn't a flight risk.

"Nope. She couldn't leave well enough alone." Tibbie pointed to herself. "Polly is mad at me for suggesting Kenni."

My head jerked to look at her.

"You're the one who told her to ask me?" I'd really thought Mama had arranged it. "I have you to thank for this?"

Jolee took her stab at me.

"At least she didn't accuse y'all of killing Lucy Ellen like she did me." Jolee shoved in her two cents.

"Did you know that she wants to go away for Christmas?" Mama's words stopped Jolee and Tibbie in their tracks. "The whole week."

Mama knew that my friends and I always spent Christmas Eve together to not only exchange gifts, but also to enjoy what we called Friendmas.

Jolee's face went blank. Her eyelashes batted up and down as she blinked in bafflement.

"You could start an argument in an empty house." I grabbed another brownie and stuffed it in my mouth too, making Mama madder and madder. "I'm an adult and can spend Christmas with whoever I want. And I'm not in the wedding because Polly Parker is mad at me for doing my job. So we don't have to worry about happy fat anymore."

I planted a stiff smile on my face and grabbed another brownie.

"As for you," I turned to Jolee, "I couldn't question you about it, because it's a conflict of interest and I wouldn't be a good sheriff if I did ask you questions myself. Of course I don't think you killed anyone. I've got Tina Bowers in the cell right this minute."

I took a quick breath.

"As for you, if you need Polly Parker's wedding to prove to potential clients that you are good at your job, maybe you shouldn't be a wedding planner." I'm sure my words stung Tibbie, but she needed more confidence in herself than that if she was going to be a successful businesswoman.

There were murmurs behind me that caught my attention. Slowly I turned around with half the brownie sticking out of my mouth. The flash of a camera nearly blinded me.

"And that's exactly how it happened." I grabbed the bottle of wine and filled up my glass, Finn's glass, and Tina's glass as I told them why I'd left the Euchre game early. "I got tired of everyone telling me I'm a bad person and now Edna Easterly is going to plaster that photo of me stuffing my face and telling Mama and Jolee off on the front page of the *Cottonwood Chronicle*."

The two of them laughed.

"I'm certainly glad you came with wine." Tina held up her glass from the other side of the bars. "I'm going to tell you that I didn't lace the fingernail polish with the cyanide and I don't know how it got in there." She held her glass out for a refill. "Have you even thought about the person who set off the alarm?"

"What alarm?" Finn asked.

"Cheree called me around eight thirty and said the shop's alarm was going off and when she went to check it, there wasn't anyone in there and nothing was missing. We get teenagers in there stealing hair color, so we just figured it was a kid."

Finn walked over to his fancy whiteboard and picked up a dry-erase marker.

He made his usual grid with suspects, motives, and evidence.

"Here we go. Craft time," Poppa joked. "I've never seen someone make so many little boxes and stars. Can't he just put it all up here and figure it out?" He pointed to his head.

"Don't put my name in the suspect category," Tina mumbled into her wine glass before taking a gulp. "What part of 'I didn't kill her' are y'all not getting?"

Finn and I looked between each other and her before we both turned back to the board, ignoring her.

"Who else can go up there?" Finn asked and pointed to the suspect column. "If you don't give us an alibi, then you stay our number one."

"What about Jolee Fischer? She said that she'd like to slip her something. She did it." Tina sounded so upbeat and positive with her thought. "You can't keep me much longer." The wine glass dangled from her fingertips.

"I've got enough evidence collected from your salon to present to a judge to keep you longer if I need to." Finn's brows rose.

Tina's eyes lowered before she sat back down on the cot.

"What about Alma Frederick?" Tina asked.

"What about her?" I asked.

"She thought she was something else since Bosco is the president of the Hunt Club. I do Alma's hair and nails." Tina made it sound like we should know who that was. She harrumphed when she realized we didn't.

"And how is this related to Lucy?" Finn asked.

"Hair." She pointed to her head. "Nails." She dangled one hand out in front of her, dared not to put down the wine glass. "Gossip all together."

"Fine. I'll write down Alma Frederick if you think we need to check her out." He looked at me. I nodded and he wrote down her name.

Tina's face brightened with each letter Finn wrote on the dry-erase board. He moved the marker over to the motive box next to Alma's name.

"Put the squeeze on her, Kenni-bug." Poppa rubbed his hands vigorously. "She's about to break. I can see it in her fidgety hands."

He was right. Tina was starting to pick at her nails, something she'd never do.

"Tell me why Alma should be on this very short list where all the evidence points to you." I picked up a marker.

"I told you I didn't kill her."

"Then tell me where you were the night of the murder. Because it's funny how your lawyer has left you here and hasn't called to check on you or even come down here to get you out." It was almost unnerving how comfortable Tina looked in the cell. "But if you'd prefer to be doing nails and hair in the big house among the real killers and criminals, I guess Cheree will have to hire someone else to buy you out."

"Buy me out?" That got her attention. She stomped over to the bars and stuck her nose through them. "No one is buying me out."

"Answer my question." I slammed the marker on the desk and raised my voice a few more decibels. "You and Lucy Ellen got into a fight. She threatened your business by telling you she was going to write that review. You put poison in the only nail polish she wanted and you let her kill herself unbeknownst to her!" I yelled louder and louder as her jaw got tighter and tenser.

Duke jumped up from his bed and the hair on his spine stood up.

"I was at massage school in Clay's Ferry!" she screamed and quickly shut her mouth. She looked like she surprised herself. She fell against the bars and melted down to the ground. "Are you happy? I'm a fraud. I didn't have a real massage license and I've been going to massage school on my days off and I had a two-day final. That's why I wasn't at the shop that night or the next day until late. I have the certificate and a roomful of people and clients to prove it."

Stunned, I eased down on the edge of my desk. My mouth dropped, my shoulders slumped. Even now that she did have an alibi the night of Lucy's death and the days leading up to it, she could still be held on fraud charges.

"Now let me go. I've got a wedding party to take care of."

She stood back up, ran her hands down her shirt and over her hair.

"Not so fast." Finn took over. He could see the shock on my face. "Now we know you're running a fraudulent business. We might be able to help you if you cooperate in this investigation."

"How?" She planted a closed fist on her hip.

"You mentioned Alma Frederick." I gathered my wits about me and pushed myself up to stand. "You tell me everything you know that's not gossip. The truth. I'll check out the truth and if it does check out, then and only then will I think about letting you out of here."

"What about the fraud charges? I have my license now." She chewed on the inside of her jaw.

"I can probably get the judge to be lenient." It wasn't going to be easy since the judge had probably been one of Tina's clients, but I was willing to try.

"Alma and Lucy Ellen hated each other. It's no secret that Darnell wants to be the Hunt Club president." Tina wagged a finger at me. "No different than a sheriff's election to them. Apparently," her voice did an upswing in tone, "Bosco and Darnell are hunting partners. When Darnell and Lucy Ellen were having problems, it tickled Alma pink because she knew the women in the Hunt Club wouldn't vote in a divorced man since their morals are so high brow." She pish-poshed their attitude.

"Darnell and Lucy Ellen were having troubles?" I asked.

Finn was busy making notes on the board while I asked the questions.

"Yes. A year or so ago. According to Alma, they are happy as two love doves now, but Alma and Lucy Ellen compete for the same nail color, same hair color, even same hairstyle." She nodded. "They come in and ask what the other one gets. I'm not going to lie, and I love Jesus. What I do might seem wrong, but I embellish some of their treatments they get."

"What do you mean?" Finn turned around.

"Say Lucy Ellen came in to get a pedicure. Well, I might tell Alma that Lucy Ellen got a pedicure and a hot stone message. Then Alma will top that service for the week," she said.

We looked at her with our jaws dropped.

"What?" she asked as if it were no big deal. "I've got to make a living. I'm upselling. All the big city salons do it."

"I'm not sure, but I don't think she knows what upselling is," I whispered to Finn. "But why would Alma want to kill Lucy?"

"They were in such competition. The last time Alma was in, she asked me about buying the same color nail polish, Perfectly Posh. I told her what I told Lucy. I don't sell it. She told me that Bosco had put her on a beauty budget, which to no end thrilled Lucy." Tina rolled her eyes. "Which made me lose money because Lucy Ellen didn't have to keep up with what Alma was doing. But regardless." She flapped her hand down in front of her. "Alma was none too happy when I wouldn't sell her the bottle. Now it's missing."

Finn and I could see where making a friendly house call to Alma Frederick wouldn't hurt anything.

"Alma knew that Perfectly Posh was Lucy's favorite. She came in and stole it. Put the cyanide in it and gave the fingernail polish to Lucy Ellen as a peace offering." Tina was getting more and more into her idea of Alma being the killer. She scooted herself up to the edge of the cot and stood up. She paced back and forth as the story came to her head, which really wasn't a bad theory. "Not only did Lucy Ellen accept her gift, she painted her nails. This way, Alma got her revenge without getting her hands dirty. Alma Frederick does not like to get her hands dirty." Tina nodded with satisfaction.

"Can I see you over here for a second, Finn?" I nodded to the corner of the room. This was when I wished we had more than a one-room department.

"What's up?" Finn bent his head toward me after we walked over near his desk, which was at the far side of the room near the back door.

"Alma might be another good lead, but I also heard from Malina that Marcy and Lucy Ellen had words. Apparently, Lucy Ellen was going on and on about how Marcy wasn't letting the citizens use their tax dollars that went toward the library when Marcy refused to let Lucy Ellen use the computers to write her reviews," I whispered so Tina didn't hear. "I questioned Marcy about it, but nothing really came of it."

"What about the polish? When does Tina make the polish?" Poppa asked after he appeared between me and Finn, ignoring the fact that Finn and I were in a conversation.

"The bottle of nail polish is something I really want in my hand," I said. "I know if we can find it, that's our murder weapon."

"How long does nail polish stay good?" Poppa asked another great question. "You need to ask her more questions about the nail polish."

"What was the mayor thing about out there?" Finn asked.

"I think it's strange that the mayor has taken a very vested interest in me not investigating. It's alarming really. Was he hiding something? I just had to know." I tried to stay focused on Finn even though Poppa's observation about the nail polish had my head swirling with thoughts.

"And?" Finn asked, his voice escalated.

"He just wants his wedding to go off without a hitch. That's all. Even though most of these people have alibis, they still could've poisoned the polish and given it to Lucy Ellen and waited until she painted her nails." Something just wasn't right about all of these suspects in my head. I had a nigglin' suspicion I was missing something. Maybe Poppa was right. There was something about the polish.

"You're right. That's why it's so important we continue to track who Lucy Ellen had been in contact with since her last nail appointment." Finn had a terrific thought.

"Tina!" I pushed past Finn. "When was the last time that you did do Lucy's nails?"

"It would be in the appointment book, but about two weeks ago. It was whenever the SPCA was having their big food drive because she's part of that program, though she doesn't have any animals."

"SPCA?" I remembered the review Lucy Ellen had written about the Pet Patch. "Lucy Ellen wrote a bad review about Pet Patch. I did go by and see her. Nothing much to say." I shrugged. "But Lucy Ellen could've made someone at the SPCA mad."

"Faith Dunaway is so good to me and Cosmo." Finn loved his cat so much. "She makes her own catnip." Finn walked over to the white board and wrote "Marcy Carver" and "SPCA."

Just when I thought I was running out of suspects, the list suddenly got a little longer.

"Sweet Marcy Carver?" Tina's mouth dropped.

"Ignore that," I told her and walked up to the cell. "As you know I'm not really up to date on manicures and all things related to girly stuff."

My words made her smile.

"Apparently," she looked at Finn and then looked back at me giving me a wink, "you snagged him and he likes whatever it is that you've got going on." She winked again.

"Focus," I instructed her. "You make the polish as needed. Why?"

"Good work, Kenni-bug." Poppa smacked his hands together and rubbed them vigorously.

"So I won't waste the ingredients." She looked at me as if I should've know that. Then it was as if a light bulb went off in her head. "I make the bottles small because not everyone loves my homemade colors. Lucy Ellen was the only person who loved my Perfectly Posh on a regular basis so I made a small bottle for her. Her bottle is only good for about a week until the ingredients separate." She was getting so excited, that her voice escalated and her chest heaved up and down as she tried to get her train of thought out.

She grabbed the bars with both hands. Her knuckles turned white she was squeezing so hard.

"Whatever polish she used wasn't made by me." Tina smiled so big. Her eyes widened. "I wouldn't have kept her bottle. I hadn't made Polly's bridal shower polish yet. I was going to make it fresh so it looked good."

"Are you saying that you threw out the bottle of Perfectly Posh you used on Lucy Ellen the last time she came in?" Finn asked.

"That's exactly what I'm saying." Tina nodded her head. "In fact, the day she came in demanding me to do her nails, I didn't have any made up. Remember how she kept looking for it while I was doing you?"

"I do," I replied and ignored Poppa who was now in the cell with Tina doing his little happy jig.

"When does your dumpster come?" Finn asked.

"It's long gone by now. That was a couple of weeks ago. And I had no time to make up any nail polish since I've been going back and forth to Clay's Ferry." She let go of the bars and crossed her arms across her chest with a huge grin on her face. "Someone other than me knows how to make my polish."

Chapter Fourteen

Even though Tina had coughed up her alibi and the fact that she said she hadn't made the polish, it was too late to get the necessary paperwork filed to let her go so late at night. Finn and I decided that he'd stay there to keep an eye on her and I'd go home to get some sleep.

But before I could do that, I headed to Clay's Ferry to drop off the evidence I'd collected at Tiny Tina's.

"Where are we headed?" Poppa asked from the passenger seat.

"Tom Geary's lab." The Wagoneer rattled down the old road toward Clay's Ferry. "The cyanide bottle and the fingernail polish from Cheree's station are my main focus. I want to see if there are fingerprints."

"This was a special circumstances case due to the nature of the murder weapon. Just because everyone seemed to have an alibi didn't mean they didn't premeditate it days or even weeks before." Poppa didn't tell me something I already didn't know. "This might be our toughest case yet."

The anxiety in his words knotted my insides.

When we got to the lab, I knew that Tom had a container in the back of the brick building that led into the building, which was under tight security. The container was for the after-hours evidence that was dropped off. It was big enough for the bottle and the other evidence bags to fit in.

I called and left Tom a voicemail. "Hi, Tom." I didn't worry with calling his after-hours service that would make him come in and process the evidence. "It's Sheriff Lowry from Cottonwood." I told him who I was, though he'd already know. Everything had to be on the up and up and nothing left undone. "I just put a couple of evidence bags in the overnight container. One has a bottle of cyanide that was found at one of the evidence scene locations and the other has some generic fingernail polish that was probably picked up at the dollar store."

I wasn't exactly sure if Cheree had truly picked up the polish there or somewhere else for a dollar, but that didn't matter.

"What I'm looking for are fingerprints. Specifically to see if there are matching prints on either. Give me a call when you get it completed." I hung the phone up and grabbed the bags out of the backseat before I got out and put them in the container.

After I'd gotten home, I spent the better part of the night tossing and turning.

Duke even got so tired of me rolling side to side that he got off the bed and slept on the floor. Not only the fact that Tina had put doubt in my head about her being the killer, but the guilt about Polly Parker and Mama had settled into the bottom of my heart.

It wasn't that I was ruthless or mean—it was the fact that the two of them expected me to do what they wanted me to do. Mama was probably more embarrassed than I was that Polly had dropped me from her wedding.

Instead of waiting for my alarm to go off at six a.m., I decided to get on up. With the coffee pot brewing, Duke let outside, and his bowl filled with kibble, I knew I had to go make amends with Polly. It wasn't until the hot shower was running over me that I got an idea that might make everyone happy. Besides, the annual gun show I needed to check out didn't start until ten and I knew Polly worked for Viola White at White's Jewelers on Fridays. The jewelry store opened at seven, giving me enough time to get ready for my day and be at the shop waiting on Polly before it opened.

White's Jewelers was located on Main Street along with the other boutique shops in Cottonwood. They were all very unique and charming in their own way. It was nice that we had the Sweet Adelines that helped keep everything nice, clean, and in order. The city council also made sure all the shops were tidy and fit the cozy small-town feel that Cottonwood was known for.

Viola White's shop had been a staple since before I was even born. She took pride in her jewelry, which made her business very personal to her and her clients. Viola was getting up in age and she only let Polly Parker work part-time for her to give herself a weekly break. Other than that, Viola was always there. Polly's day was Friday and it being so close to her wedding, a little more than a week away, I was hoping she didn't take off.

The awning over the shop flapped in the cool breeze that shuffled its way down Main Street. The grey awning that had "White's Jewelry" scrolled in calligraphy with two white illustrated diamonds on each side of the name hung evenly over the two large windows that looked right into the shop.

It brightened my day to see Polly Parker in there going through the glass jewelry counters trying on all the fancy rings and holding them out to look at.

"My oh my." Polly Parker's voice dripped of Southern charm when Duke and I walked in. "Look what the cat dragged in so early this morning."

"Polly." I stepped up to the counter. "I know I'm the last person on this earth you want to see, but I've got an idea that might make you happy."

"I've got nothing good to say to you, Kenni Lowry. You have not only stepped on my heart, but you've smashed it into the ground with those boots you wear." Her words made me look down at my feet.

Yeah, so I wore cowboy boots every single day with my uniform. They were comfortable. Duke sniffed my boots as if he knew exactly what she'd said. He looked up at me with those big round brown eyes. I patted his head.

"I'm sorry, Polly. I truly am, but I can't just ignore the law and the crimes committed so I can be your maid of honor." This sure wasn't going as it had in my head while I was in the shower, so I took a deep breath and collected my thoughts. "I have a job to do like you've got a job to do here."

"What is it you want?" Those pretty little blue eyes glared at me before they shifted to Duke as he lay by my feet.

"I know that you're mad because I have Tina Bowers in the county jail and she can't do all the nails of the girls in your bridal party because she's locked up. But she might be out before your nail party tonight. I promise to let you know in a couple of hours." That was the long and short of why she was mad at me. "If what I'm thinking doesn't pan out, what if I let you and your bridal party come down to the department tonight and let Tina do your nails there?"

"Kenni." Polly's voice choked. She brought her hand up to her chest. "You'd do that for little ole me?"

Now she was going to play the poor pitiful Southern belle on me.

"I think it's a way to make you happy and my mama happy. Let's face it." It was time to come clean. "You don't care that

Tina Bowers is under arrest for killing someone. You probably only invited her to your wedding because your mama made you." Polly's eyes started to lower. "Don't be going and glaring at me. You know I'm right. You only care that the nails of your wedding party are all done the same and Tina is cheap."

"Yeah, so?" she snarled.

"This way, we both get what we want. You get your nails done. Tina gets paid handsomely by you." I threw that part in because I knew Tina was losing money sitting in jail and I still had my doubts she killed Lucy. "And I'm still your maid of honor."

Duke groaned and rolled to his side.

"Deal." She gave me her word, which was better than a handshake in the South. "Thank goodness, because Mama was going to Blanche's to get fitted for your dress. I was going to have to use my own mama for my maid of honor."

"You should've asked Toots." I gave her another chance to back out of asking me.

"I couldn't ask her. I don't want her to feel obligated to pay that much for a dress when I really want her to enjoy herself." Polly at least looked out for her friend.

"You go on and tell Tibbie that we made up. Then you show up tonight at the department around seven for a nail painting party if you haven't heard from me." It all sounded good until Tina flipped her lid when I got back to the department and told her my idea when Duke and I showed up to relieve Finn since there was still an hour before I had to leave for the gun show and Betty got to work.

"Nail painting party in jail?" She stuck her nose between the bars of the cell.

I thought it was a pretty good idea, however apparently Tina didn't like my thoughts. Finn said he was going to head over to Clay's Ferry to check out Tina's alibi before he went home. I'd expected to hear from him within the hour.

"You agreed to this?" she asked me.

"I came up with the idea." I shrugged, thinking I'd really done something for everyone. "I told her that she had to pay you extra. But this is only if your alibi doesn't pan out."

"No matter what your mama says, you go on and have a great Christmas with that man." Tina winked.

"How did you know about the Christmas thing?" I asked.

"Viv stopped by this morning. She gave Finn all sort of business for asking you to come to meet his parents. It's obvious she thinks you are required to spend every single second of every single holiday, including Arbor Day, here in Cottonwood."

"Mama," I groaned. She was going to mess up anything I had with Finn if I didn't put a stop to her nonsense. I thought she'd come to grips with me going, not the same as okay, but she did seem that she accepted the fact I was going to Chicago.

"Come on, Kenni." Tina waved me over. "Come play cards with me until Finn calls with my alibi."

"I'm not playing cards with you. I'm going to the gun show so I can have a little visit with Alma while you stay here with Betty," I said just as Betty came through the door.

Her pink hair rollers were still in her hair, which wasn't unusual since she believed the longer she left them in, the longer they'd set for her plans later in the day. She had on her usual house dress with her pocketbook hanging from the crook of her arm.

"Tina Bowers." Betty acted surprised. "What on earth?"

"Oh, shut up." Tina snarled. "I know all y'all nosy women on the church telephone list have already tried and hung me for Lucy's murder."

Betty's mouth opened to protest but quickly snapped shut

when she realized Tina was right. She scurried over to her desk and put her pocketbook down. She fluffed the pillow in her chair before she sat down. The chair creaked in protest. Though she seemed to be minding her own business, she was doing a busy job of minding mine too.

"I've got an alibi. Go on," she baited Betty, "ask Kenni what my alibi is so you can go and spread it around town."

"You've lost your mind sitting in there all night." Betty rolled her eyes.

Tina motioned for Betty to come closer. "Now, dig down in that pocketbook of yours and get me a piece of gum. You've always got gum when you come see me."

Betty dug deep in her purse and retrieved a piece of crumpled-up gum that'd seen better days. Without even brushing off the specks of God knows what on it, Tina stuck it in her mouth. Betty walked over to Cowboy's.

"So is there anything else you can remember since last night about Alma's relationship with Lucy?" I asked.

"There was something." Tina perked up when she saw Betty bring in a pot of coffee from next door. "Can I get a cup of that coffee? Thank you, Betty. I'm sorry I fussed at you a while ago." She gave a theatrical wink that made me roll my eyes. "As I was sayin', I'd heard that Lucy Ellen got drunk at their last hog boil and Alma found her and Bosco in the barn doing more than talking pig, if you know what I mean."

"Now I heard the complete opposite." Betty couldn't stand it. She had to get her two cents in. She got up and got a cup of the coffee. As she ripped open a few sugar packets and stirred it, she said, "Lucy Ellen told the girls at bell choir that Alma had hit on Darnell. When Darnell rejected her, she went and told Bosco that Darnell hit on her and they got into a big fight and that's why they aren't friends no more."

"I thought they were hunting partners." I glanced over at the whiteboard where we'd written that supposed fact.

"Apparently they don't go to the deer stand the same nights and have switched partners." Betty shrugged.

"Why haven't you told me this information before now?" I asked and wondered who was at the cabin the night of the murder. If Bosco and Darnell didn't go the same time, where was Bosco Frederick that night?

"Because you always tell me the proof is in the evidence and not gossip," Betty jabbed back. "The evidence clearly points right to Tina."

"Gee, thanks, Betty. I have an alibi. Just wait and see when Finn calls." Tina huffed. "When I get out of here, you're gonna regret saying that when you need to get them gnarly corns on your feet sawed down. Besides, Alma was just in the salon to have her nails manicured and painted. She still holds a grudge against Lucy."

"I've told you time and time again that there's some truth in all gossip and you've got to weed it out." Poppa appeared next to the whiteboard. "I'd go see the Fredericks as soon as possible."

The phone rang and Betty quickly answered.

"Hold on." She held it out to me. "It's Officer Vincent."

Tina bounced with anticipation on her toes.

"Hey, Finn. What did you find out?" I asked.

"Tina's alibi holds true. She was doing a massage therapist test up until nine p.m. and after that they went out for a late supper and ended up watching a movie well into the night. Airtight. And her prints haven't been found on the bottle."

"Sounds good." I looked over at Tina, knowing that the alibi wasn't as important since she could've poisoned the fingernail polish at anytime. I really needed to figure out how Lucy Ellen got the polish.

"Well?" she asked.

"You're okay with me going to get some shut eye?" Finn asked. He sounded tired.

"Yeah. Go on home. I'll have Betty call Wally Lamb to pick Tina up." I could hear Tina give a little yelp. "I've got a lot to get done. I'm going to head on over to the gun show at The Moose Lodge to see what's going on there."

We hung up the phone.

"Aren't they gonna have the cutest babies?" Tina asked Betty.

"Her mama already has the names picked out," Betty said. When I gave her a cross look, she followed up by saying, "That's just hearsay and as you can see, hearsay isn't always the truth."

"The truth is what I seek." I grabbed my bag and made sure I had everything I needed. "I'm going to go see Alma Frederick. Be sure to call Tibbie Bell to let her know that you're still going to be at Mama's tonight for the bridal supper."

Mama's bridal supper was the last place I wanted to spend my Friday night. But the way I saw it, in seven days this wedding and hopefully this investigation would both be over and in the rearview mirror of my life.

Chapter Fifteen

Duke beat me to the Wagoneer. He was ready to go for a ride no matter where we were headed.

"Alright, buddy." I rolled down the windows to let in the fall breeze. "Let's go to a gun show."

There were a couple of cars in the parking lot next to the metal building with big black letters on the side that read "The Moose."

The Moose was a great source of pride in Kentucky. The Moose Lodge was founded in Louisville, Kentucky in the late nineteenth century. It was an organization that gave back to their community. Mostly made of men, but some women. Of course, there was a bar that served super cheap drinks and had a band on the weekends, but as for the giving, they gave so much to Cottonwood. They volunteered in the school system and did many fundraising events for our small town.

There was nothing Mama loved more than a good Moose holiday dance, which was coming up. The Christmas dance was a big deal around here and there was even a Christmas Queen crowned for one of the elder women in the community. It was a sight to see. Truly.

"You coming?" I held the door and looked at Duke.

He jumped over into the driver's seat and hopped out. Soon

the parking lot would be full. Everyone loved a good gun show and in the end, it helped them put on the dance, where all the proceeds went to help the needy families in Cottonwood and the local schools.

"Hey there, Sheriff," one of the women at the door greeted me from behind a card table. "We've got all the necessary paperwork to have all the artillery in here."

She flipped open a metal box that had a plastic tray for money. She lifted the tray up and dug through until she found an envelope that had the necessary permits from the clerk's office.

"Here you go." She handed them to me. She pointed to the doors I'd just walked through. "We've got the signs posted as well."

Not that I was there for that, but it sure did give me a good reason to start snooping around for Alma and Bosco Frederick. The gun show was held in the recreation area where there was a big basketball court. Many of the youth used it for the local summer camps and it was perfectly set up today with display cases full of guns, tables, and even a sort of museum that told the history of Cottonwood, hunting, and The Moose's contribution to the community.

"Is your president still Bosco?" I asked.

"It sure is. His wife is right over there." She waved a hand in the air. "Alma! Allllllma!" she hollered and got the attention of a woman with a blonde bob haircut that flipped up at the ends all around her head. The top and sides of her hair were flattened down to her head.

When she walked over, I noticed her polyester brown pants, brown shirt, and white cardigan along with her very sensible brown shoes. She looked like she competed with Lucy. I could definitely see the uptight resemblance.

"Sheriff," Alma greeted me with a grin. She stuck her hand out to shake mine and I couldn't help but notice the big diamond that rested on the top of her ring finger. It had to be the one Viola White had mentioned Bosco had bought Alma.

Alma was a much older lady than Lucy Ellen and I'd put her in her late sixties, if not seventies. The wrinkles on her hand and neck were much more than I'd expected to see. "I'm sure you'll find everything in order. My husband has worked nonstop to get everything together for this year's annual show. Which, as you know, helps fund the Christmas dance."

I couldn't help but notice that her nails weren't painted. Didn't Tina tell me that Alma had just been into the salon to get them manicured?

"Yes. And the department thanks you for your kind service since I know that you do this out of the goodness of your heart." I took out the paperwork and pretended to look through it so she'd buy that I was there for that purpose. "Is your husband here?"

I held the papers toward her and pointed to his signature.

"Heavens to Betsy, no." She giggled like I should know that. "Miss the first two weeks of getting the cabin and stand ready? The weather was perfect for a big hog hunt and he's not about to miss out on that."

"That's right. I'd heard about that from Darnell Lowell." My chin drew down and I shook my head. "Shame about Lucy."

Alma hummed but said nothing more.

"I guess you and Lucy Ellen were friends since everyone here gets along so well." It was a simple statement that made her react with a big inhale that caught my attention. Maybe there was something to this gossip Tina and Betty had talked about.

Like Poppa always said, when it came to gossip and fact,

there's some truth in between the two somewhere; you've just got to pick it apart and find it.

"I wouldn't call us friends." Her words had a bit of a sour bite to them.

"Really?" My head shifted to the side. "I'd heard y'all were pretty good friends since your husbands shared a deer stand together."

"Just because they share a deer stand doesn't mean they share everything. And they stopped sharing recently," she said, giving Duke a pat on the head. She was as calm as a millpond.

Duke found her boring after a couple of sniffs and took off toward another woman who offered a much better scratch behind the ear than Alma did.

I was getting the sense that she knew I wasn't there for the permit anymore.

"Of course, we were Ladies of the Moose together and had some of the same friends, but outside of that we weren't as tight as some would think." Her chest lifted along with the tip of her chin. "I feel terrible about what happened, but I'm sure Darnell feels worse."

"Yes. He's devastated. I'm sad to think that he and your husband aren't best friends, because he could use a friend right now. He is already very lonely." It was a mere suggestion to see if there were any sort of reaction to hint toward what Betty had said about Alma and Darnell having an affair.

"Jail will do that to you..." Her voice trailed off.

"Jail?" I asked.

"Isn't Darnell in jail?" she asked. When I looked at her funny, she said, "For killing Lucy."

"Why on earth would you think that?" I asked.

"Oh dear." She waved her hand toward me and got a bit teary eyed. "I'd heard Darnell and Lucy Ellen were having a big fight about the wedding."

The wedding. My jaw clenched just thinking about it.

"Yes. He said that she wanted him to go, but he told her no because he wanted to go hunting."

My lips pinched together and flattened out across my face. "Who told you that?"

"Bosco. He said that it was all the talk at the cabin that night. So when he went home, we figured they got into a fight." She shrugged. "It's still a tragedy."

"What about their relationship?" I asked and wondered if Bosco had told her all that when in reality he was at the Lowell house pursuing an affair with Lucy. But how would he have poisoned her with the polish?

"Why are you asking me?" she questioned. "How would I know?"

"I was thinking that maybe you and Darnell might've been a little more than just acquaintances." There. I said it. I practically accused the woman of having an affair.

"I see the sheriff has a very active imagination along with the rest of Lucy's friends. And they're supposed to be church women. They're the worst." She looked me square in the face with a dead-eyed stare. "I think it's time for me to go work on my display. If you or the department are in the market for some real guns," her eyes drew down my uniform and stopped at my holster, "y'all should come on over to my booth and buy some. Of course, it all goes to a good cause, just like we all here at the Moose do for our small town. I'll be here all day long. Not going nowhere."

"And we appreciate all the lodge does. My mama and daddy wouldn't miss the Christmas dance for nothin'." I tipped my head and excused myself. I patted my thigh. "Here, Duke," I called.

Stares and whispers greeted my back when I walked out the door. I'd done what I wanted to do there: put a bug in the ear of the Hunt Club women where I knew the gossip would trickle around. When we got back into the Jeep, there was a text from Tibbie. Not only had she thanked me for making amends with Polly, she told me to go back to Blanche's for a final fitting so Blanche would have a week to get my dress fixed. Then she texted she'd see me tonight at Mama's.

"You should be sleeping," I said to Finn when he called on my way to Blanche's.

"I can't sleep. I can't stop thinking about this case." The determination in his tone told me to not even try to get him to rest. "I really want to go back to the Lowell house and check out everything again."

"I haven't been there to clear it, so why don't we meet up there after I go for my final dress fitting?" I asked.

"Sounds good."

"And I also wanted to know if you wanted to go to the woods tonight." I had an idea.

"Huh?" The city slicker was stumped.

"I think we need to go out and take a look around those hunting woods, maybe check up on Bosco Frederick and see if all those rumors about him and Lucy Ellen were true." If Bosco wasn't coming home, I was going to go to him. I quickly filled Finn in on what I'd heard about Bosco's meandering ways.

"Are you buying into all that cheating stuff?" he asked.

"I went to see Alma and she was very uncomfortable with me asking questions. She mentioned that Bosco had told her about the fight between Lucy Ellen and Darnell. He said Darnell had mentioned it but in another breath said they weren't friends. Why would Darnell tell Bosco something so personal?" I asked. "She also said Darnell was gone from the cabin and fighting with Bosco, but Darnell told us he was at the cabin. I'm wondering if the truth about Bosco and Lucy's affair was about to come out."

"And it was Bosco who wasn't at the cabin and Lucy Ellen told him about the fight between her and Darnell." Finn read my mind.

"That's what I'm thinking." I agreed.

"No wonder you two make such a good team." Poppa sat in the front seat with a big grin on his face. "He's not so bad, I guess."

Chapter Sixteen

"Blanche?" I'd knocked on the door a couple of times and no one answered. "You stay," I called back to Duke, whose head was stuck out the window enjoying the cooler weather.

I walked around the side of the house when I heard some music. "Blanche?" I called in the direction of the vegetable garden that looked like it'd seen better days.

"Kenni, honey." Blanche stood up with a fistful of weeds in both hands. She dropped them and made her way toward me. "Do you think I'll ever get this garden winterized?"

"I know you can." There wasn't a single doubt in my mind that whatever Blanche set her mind to, she did.

"Every year I say that I'm not going to do another garden, but then I forget." She tapped her finger to her temple. "Maybe I just need a swift kick in the you-know-what when it comes spring and planting a garden."

She curled her fingers in the crook of my arm and we started walking toward the house.

"I hear you're back in the wedding party." She squeezed her fingers and used her other hand to pat my arm. "If we ever get this girl married off, we'll be doing good. But I fear she's taking this First Lady of Cottonwood thing too far."

She opened the screen door that led into her porch. The

dress rack with all the wedding party dresses that was in the bedroom had been moved here.

"How so?" I asked and stepped inside.

"She's now wanting to be introduced by Preacher Bing as the Mayor and First Lady." Blanche tsked and walked over to the rack, pulling out the green dress. "This sure is ugly."

"It's her dream to have a *Gone with the Wind* theme." I bit my lip to stop any sort of gossip about Polly's wedding. The last thing I needed was to get kicked out again. "I just wish I'd gotten that dress instead."

The red one on the hanger was much more flattering.

"How's it going, sweetie?" she asked out of concern.

"Mama and I still haven't talked much about Christmas and I figure it's a couple of months away, so I'll let her let the idea sink in her head for a few weeks and then I'll just tell her that I've got my plane ticket and I'm going." It sounded so simple and easy, but the thought made me nearly sick to my stomach. Mama was never easy.

"Your mama will come around." She took the green dress off the hanger. "I've pinned and added some material here." She patted her hips as if that's where the happy fat had decided it was happiest. "And a little here." She patted her stomach.

"If I wanted to get insulted, I'd have called Mama," I joked and took the dress she was thrusting toward me.

"You can just throw it on right here." She twisted around. "No one is around. Besides, I want to hear all about Lucy Ellen while it's just me and you."

"There's not much to tell." I knew I had to keep most of the investigation close to the vest. I slipped the dress over my head and slipped out of my clothes, letting the big ole dress cover me. "I'm still trying to follow leads and talk to people who didn't think the best of her."

"Have you checked out them women at the Hunt Club?" She cocked a brow and gestured for me to turn around. She zipped the dress up. "They're all swappin' husbands and cheating and stuff." Her shoulders jerked when she let out a laugh. "They all worry about me stealing their men, when it's right underneath their noses."

Did Blanche know something that might be a lead?

"I thought the same thing and stopped by the gun show on my way over. Of course the women were all sad about Lucy, which is natural," I added just for empathy's sake.

"Yeah, right." The sarcasm was apparent in Blanche's tone. "They don't care about each other. I do all their alterations."

"Really?" I asked. "And?"

Blanche's eyes shifted sideways to look at me, but her face stayed turned to the dress. She gave a slight smile.

"And they have all their private functions at that cabin that's situated in the middle of all them deer stands. From what I heard, Art Baskin and Danny Shane not only built it for the club, but they put in security cameras in case someone came in and trashed the place. Darnell and Bosco were fighting over who was going to pay for their share. Darnell claimed he did all the taxidermy for cheap where Bosco did nothing." She let out a deep breath. "Now, that's just what I heard while I was pinning up Danny's wife's dress for the wedding."

She referred to Art Baskin, the owner of the only security system store in Cottonwood, and Danny Shane, owner of Shane Construction.

"She told you this?" I asked but didn't make eye contact.

It was an unwritten law that if there was some knowledge, in this case gossip, being spread, eye contact while telling the tale made it more solid. And no one in Cottonwood would ever get caught gossiping. Right.

"Sheila Shane was on the phone and I can't help but overhear things." She brushed her hands along the fabric around my waistline and down my hips. She took a step back. Her head tilted to the left and to the right as if she were getting perspective of her handiwork and how it fit me. "And there was some talk that they'd never know the truth behind the fight between Darnell and Bosco because the only witness was now dead."

"Lucy?" I questioned.

"Honey, it looks so good now." She drew up her chin up to my face, her eyes followed. She gave a sweet smile that told me she wasn't going to confirm my question, but I knew I was right.

"Well, I better get going." I turned back around to let her unzip me. "I left Duke in the car. He's probably ready to get going."

"The dress looks so much better." She bent down and picked my clothes up off the floor since the dress and crinoline made it hard for me to even move. "Now, you take it home and next week a couple of days before the wedding, I'm gonna have you try it on again before I quickly sew it in place."

I slipped my jeans up my legs and took the dress up over my head to put my sheriff's shirt back on.

"What do I owe you?" I asked.

"Just find out who killed Lucy Ellen Lowell. Not that she and I were best friends, but she does deserve to rest in peace." She patted my hand. "You come back and tell me what happens with your mama and Christmas." She winked and walked me outside of her house, making her way back to her garden.

I hurried to the car with the dress draped over my forearm.

"Good boy," I said to Duke and shoved the dress behind me in the backseat. I patted Duke's head and he gave me a couple of good kisses. "We've got to go make a stop to see Bosco

Frederick."

"That's what I'm talking about." Poppa appeared in the front seat of the Jeep.

Duke jumped to the back.

"Duke." I reached around and tugged on the dress but Duke didn't budge. "Can you get off?"

"He ain't gonna hurt that ugly thing." Poppa's nose curled.

"I guess you're right." I turned the engine over and pulled down Second Street.

The dress was the last thing on my mind now that it fit. It was Blanche's story that had me raring to go. I drew out on my cell and called Art Baskin. He'd worked with me on a couple cases before and I wanted to get his take on what Blanche had told me about the argument between Bosco and Darnell.

"Hi there," I said when someone answered the phone of Art's office. "This is Sheriff Kenni Lowry and I wanted to speak to Art."

"He's not here right now. Actually, he won't be here for a few days. He's gone hunting." The lady told me. "But I'll leave a message for him if he calls in."

"That'd be great. Thanks." I hung up. I scrolled through my phone. I'd called Danny Shane a couple times about his construction business as well as his dairy farm. "Hello, this is Sheriff Kenni Lowry. Can I please speak to Danny?"

"I'm sorry. He's on vacation this week." His secretary was a lot more discreet than Art's. "I'll tell him you called, unless this is an emergency? Then I can put you through to Sandy."

"No thanks. I'll just wait to talk to Danny." I clicked off my phone.

"We are on our way to Darnell's." I tapped the wheel in anticipation for the stoplight to change so I could turn left out of Second Street and then take a right on Main. "But first I want to drop Duke off at the department."

The thought of the murder sprinkled goosebumps along my neck.

"The question I keep going back to is who is framing Tina." I looked over at Poppa. His stare were haunting.

The next hour I spent going through the Lowell house with permission of Darnell. I picked up couch cushions, went through Lucy's car and all of the beds and drawers, plus the basement, and literally found nothing. Finn was right. It was as if the killer and any sort of crime had vanished. I'd even looked for the bottle of pills Darnell told me Lucy Ellen had been taking since Camille didn't seem to know when I asked her about it at Blanche's house. Camille said that Lucy Ellen didn't have high blood pressure or any other illness. What was she taking?

I flipped on the light to Darnell's work building, which was just a detached garage behind their house. The beady eyes of mounted deer heads, bucks, raccoons, and other critters with their mouths open, teeth showing, stared back at me. It was an unsettling feeling being here and knowing they'd met their demise from someone actually stalking and hunting them, sort of like the person who wanted Lucy Ellen dead.

I stepped inside to take a look around. Not that I thought Darnell had even thought to kill his wife, much less put cyanide in her fingernail polish, but just like Poppa said, no stone unturned until we find the killer.

The unsnapping of my flashlight holder echoed through the garage as I curled up on my tiptoes to shine the light into the animals' mouths in case something was hidden.

"The killer doesn't want to be found out." Poppa scared me out of my skin.

I jumped around with a tight grip on the handle of the black flashlight.

"Poppa! What happened to letting me know you were coming?" I asked.

"We've gone over this," he said flatly. "I've shown up unannounced and this is how you react. I've shown up announced and this is how you react. It seems to me that it's you who needs to be more observant."

"Whatever." I eyeballed him. "You never told me what happened at Dixon's."

"Just a bunch of rowdy preteen boys that needed a little scaring. If they don't get scared now, they will be the next criminals." He laughed. "I'm kinda liking this ghost thing. I untied one of the boy's shoes and stepped on the shoelace with one foot and did the same to the boy standing next to him. When I sent the candy flying off the shelf, they looked at each other and tried to take off running. Then tripped all over one another because I was standing on some shoelaces."

This was a different side of Poppa that he rarely showed. When he was living, he was so focused on the job and not living life. Being a ghost brought out the playful side in him and I enjoyed seeing it.

"Heathens," he spat, and both of us laughed.

There were a few of those cardboard boxes that stored printer paper with "photos" written in Sharpie stored on one of the wire shelves.

"Yeah. There's a lot of heathens around here lately." I slid the lid off and started going through the memories Darnell was holding onto.

There were photos as far back as their wedding. Lucy Ellen sure did make a beautiful bride. Looking at her made me think of Polly. I really should be much more involved and nicer than I'd been. After all, it was her big day.

The beach pictures of her and Darnell were sweet. They

were smiling and laughing. Though they never had children, they did look like they really enjoyed themselves.

"Whoa, look at that." Poppa was looking over my shoulder. "They sure were good friends."

Darnell and Bosco were in some hunting photos holding their trophies up by the antlers.

"And vacations?" he asked when I continued to thumb through more photos of Lucy, Darnell, Bosco and Alma together on what looked like a cruise, at casinos, and on the beach.

"And look at this one." I held up one where Lucy Ellen was sitting on Darnell's lap and Alma was glaring at them. Bosco must've taken it. "And this one."

There were several photos where Alma was not the happy one in the photos.

"And she told me they weren't friends." I let out a long deep breath. "I've got to go see Bosco Frederick. I wonder if he's at home."

"Only one way to find out." Poppa was thinking what I was thinking.

"With Alma at the gun show, maybe he's home, so we'll check there first." I stuck a couple of the photos in my pocket and put the lid back on the box before I slid it back into place on the wire rack. "If he's not there, we might have to go to the woods." I looked over at Duke. "I'm going to take you to the department first."

Within a couple of minutes, we'd pulled in front of Cowboy's Catfish in the open parking space, which was rare, so I took it.

Laughter spilling out of The Tattered Cover Books and Inn caught my attention. Darnell had said he was staying there and a quick stop in to ask him about the photos wouldn't hurt. I needed to get down to the truth about the friendship Alma and

Lucy Ellen had and why Alma was going to great lengths to cover it up.

Duke and I trotted across the street like a game of Frogger. The Tattered Cover Books and Inn, Tattered Cover for short, was one of two places to stay while visiting Cottonwood. The other was The Inn and it was located near the river. So you could choose to enjoy the downtown shops and eateries if you stayed at The Tattered Cover or the beautiful Kentucky scenery and landscape the country had to offer at The Inn.

"You stay out here," I instructed Duke. He wasn't very fond of cats and Purdy was the mascot of the hotel.

Nanette was sitting with Darnell in what I called the refreshment room, to the right as soon as you walked through the front door. Nanette was the owner and operator of the hotel and she took great pride in offering refreshments and cold iced tea to her inn guests.

"Lucy Ellen did love cats." Darnell rubbed down Purdy, the feline curled up on his lap.

"You know if there's anything I can do to make your stay more comfortable, you just have to blink. Not even ask." Nanette stood up. She gave me a sympathetic smile when she noticed I'd walked into the room.

"Hi, Kenni." When she said my name, Darnell looked up. The sudden jerk must've scared Purdy because she bolted off his lap.

"Hello, Nanette." I gestured to Darnell. "I wanted to come by and ask Darnell a few questions. Do you mind leaving us alone for a minute?" I asked.

"Sure." Nanette nodded and walked backward toward the hallway. "I can even shut the double doors so no one else will interrupt you."

She moved back a couple of the wing-backed chairs that

helped keep the doors propped open and quietly shut the doors behind her.

"Do you have any news?" Darnell asked.

"Nothing yet, but I wanted to know about these." I pulled the photos out for him to look at.

He cracked a weak smile and gave a slight nod of his head.

"Those were the days." He flipped through them again before handing them back to me. "The four of us were good friends in our younger days. Me and Bosco used to be hunting partners, but Alma put an end to that."

"How?" I asked.

"She started to do some really weird things, like sabotage things Lucy Ellen would do for the club. The members of the club, we like to get together. Lucy Ellen had prepared all the meat for one of them get-togethers and it was all the meat from our freezer. Alma ended up bringing Bosco's meat." He looked down at his hand and twirled his wedding band.

"I don't understand."

"It's a big deal to have your meat featured at a cookout and all your buddies eat it. Lucy Ellen loved to prepare my meats in a fancy marinade and sauce. Bosco didn't let Alma prepare his meat. But Alma couldn't stand that my meat was going to be featured and when she pulled out their meat, Lucy Ellen lost it. She didn't understand why Alma would do such a thing when there was an unwritten rule."

"I see." I eased up to the edge of the chair. "Are you okay?"

His hands were shaking, he looked up with wet eyes, his lips curled in, his chest jerked as he tried to fight back tears.

"I never thought of Alma hurting my Lucy Ellen until now." His voice cracked. "Do you think she did it?"

"I'm not sure. But I'm looking at everyone." I patted his leg. "Did you know of any other tension between the two women?"

"That was the beginning of this crazy notion that Lucy Ellen had to compete with Alma. Lucy Ellen started doing weird shopping and wanting all sorts of crazy things done to her body like..." He started to tap his head.

"Botox?" I asked.

"Yes. Lucy Ellen said she talked to Camille about it. I told her no. That she was beautiful the way she was and she said that she didn't want to look older than she was. I told her she was acting nuts." He gulped.

"I talked to Camille and she didn't say anything about Botox, but she did say that Lucy Ellen didn't have high blood pressure or any other illness. You said..." I took my notebook out of the front pocket of my shirt and started to flip through it. "Where is it?"

I continued to flip until I got to the page.

"Here." I read off my notes from the initial investigation. "You said that she was taking a pill. Do you know what pill that was?"

"No clue." He shrugged.

"I couldn't find any pills at the house and Camille said it could be a vitamin. Did she take vitamins?" I asked.

"I'm not sure. She took care of any medical things. If I got a cold, she took care of me and I swallowed whatever she gave me."

I smiled at his words.

"Who's going to take care of me now?" He put his head into his hands and began to sob. "Who would do this?"

"I'm not sure." I rubbed his back and sat with him for a few minutes until his crying stopped.

"I'm sorry. I know I shouldn't be crying like a baby, but me and Lucy, we don't have no kids and no family here. My brother down in Tulsa said I could come live with him and his family, but that's just not home." He wiped his face with the sleeve of his shirt. "I've got an appointment with Max today to make arrangements for the funeral."

I wanted to tell him to steer clear of next weekend's Parker wedding, but I figured Max would know all of that.

"I've taken up enough of your time. If you remember anything specific about Alma and Lucy, let me know." I stood up. "One more question. What did Bosco think of all this nonsense between your wives?"

"He said that we couldn't be partners anymore. He said that Alma continued to ask him to find out what Lucy Ellen was doing or where she was during the day, clubs she was in outside of the Hunt Club. It was weird, so he said that it was best we didn't hang out anymore because it drove his wife crazy and she was driving him crazy." He sniffed.

"Thanks, Darnell. I'll be in touch." I opened the double doors and waved to Nanette on my way out of the hotel.

"Good boy." I patted Duke on the head. He'd stayed exactly where I told him to. He was such a good boy.

We crossed the street and headed on back to Cowboy's Catfish.

The restaurant was busy and so was the staff. Duke and I headed on back to the office, though Duke did make a small detour to the many outstretched hands that summoned him over for a pat. He was a sucker for those fingers.

"Thank gawd you're back." Tina jumped up from the cot and stuck the center of her face in between the bars. "I've got to get a shower before tonight. I've got an alibi. This is ridiculous."

"Kenni, she's driving me crazy." Betty raised her hand in the air, extended her fingers, and make the talking gesture.

I looked between them. Betty's face was pinched and stressed.

"Wally hasn't come to get her yet?" I asked.

"Nope," Betty griped.

"I was going to leave Duke here, but I guess he can go with me. I can drop Tina off." I knew it was unconventional and her lawyer should come get her, but Cottonwood and our department was unconventional.

"Great. And," she handed me a piece of paper, "call your mama."

I tucked the piece of paper in my back pocket and walked over to the cell. I twisted the handle.

"You mean to tell me this wasn't locked?" Tina stepped out.

"Nah." I put my hand on my utility belt. "Betty, can you pull up Bosco Frederick's address?"

"I know where they live." Tina sucked in a deep breath. "Freedom sure does smell good."

"You know how to get there?" I asked.

"I had to go out there once when Alma had the Hunt Club ladies over for a spa day. I'm not gonna say it's far, but I had to grease the wagon twice before I hit the main road." Her lips duck-billed.

"That far?" My shoulders slumped. I wished I would've let Wally get her now because I didn't want her to talk my ear off.

She nodded.

"I've got plenty of time to show you." She smiled, knowing it was some good gossip.

"Did you get a lead?" Betty asked. She leaned in. Her face didn't look so stressed as she craned her neck to listen.

"Let's go. But you're staying in the car." I warned Tina and jerked my head to the side. "Come on, Duke."

Betty flipped him a treat on our way out.

"Why you going to see Bosco? And is that your dress for Polly's wedding back there?" Tina yammered on and on before I could even answer one question.

"It's not any of your business why I'm going to see him. You're going to just sit there and not say a word." I headed on out of town.

Duke continued to try and push his way up to Tina's seat.

"He's alright, really." Tina lifted her hand and patted him. She tried to be nice, but after the fifth time she pushed him back. "He just wants to give me some lovin'."

"Duke, back." My voice was a little more forceful and he knew I meant it.

I glanced in the rearview mirror. Duke was sitting on the dress and Poppa was right next to him.

Tina was right. It was a far piece out to the Frederick house. The only good thing about driving this far was how Mother Nature had painted the landscape with her beautiful foliage. The stone slave walls hugged the road on each side and the leaves were losing their green touches to early signs of vibrant oranges, reds, and golds.

"How did your visit to the Moose go?" Tina asked, knowing I'd gone there to check on her story.

"I saw Alma and she claims that she and the Lowells were never good friends. Especially her and Lucy." The Jeep curved the country road like a glove.

"She's lying. At least they were friends until all the cheating occurred," she protested.

"Do you know for sure if they cheated?" I asked.

"Not for sure, but I do know they were friends. Good friends. When I came out here to do the spa day for the women, Lucy Ellen insisted that she pay for it. Which she did. She and Alma did that back-and-forth no-I'll-pay or at-least-let-me-pay-half conversation until Lucy Ellen finally gave in and let Alma pay for it. Granted, Lucy Ellen bragged on how much money she and Darnell have and I don't think that sat well with Alma." Her jaw dropped. "You know what?" she gasped. "It was then that the two started competing for spa treatments. Lucy Ellen did back down to a couple of times a month and then she'd miss appointments or cancel them all together."

"When was this again?" I asked.

"During the summer. I can go back through my calendar at the shop and give you an exact date." She continued to give me directions by finger pointing to turn here and yonder until we made it.

The Fredericks' house sat on a bit of land going east out of town into the deep country. The view was unbelievable.

"I thought you said they didn't have as much money as the Lowells?" I knew this was a million-dollar view.

"I didn't say that. I said that Lucy Ellen said that to me when she'd come into the spa. If you ask me, I think it was the other way around and Lucy Ellen only bragged to make it look like they had money." She continued to stare out the window. "I thought you said you talked to Alma this morning."

"I did, why?" I asked.

"Why on earth would she come back here if she was going to spend the day at the Moose?" she asked.

"Where is she?" I looked out the windshield expecting to see Alma.

"I guess inside, but that's her car and Bosco's truck." She brought my attention to the two vehicles parked on the side of the house.

"You stay here." I looked at her and Duke. "I'll leave the windows down for air."

Poppa walked next to me as we made our way up the front steps of the cabin and onto the covered porch. Being nosy, I walked to the right side of the porch and noticed it wrapped all the way around. Poppa had already disappeared. On my way back to the front door to ring the doorbell, Poppa appeared. His face was faded even more than his normal ghost self.

"What's wrong?" I asked him.

"Kenni, call for backup. They're dead." His words sent a shockwave through me.

Chapter Seventeen

"Betty." My voice cracked when I spoke into the walkie-talkie, "I...um..."

"Y'alright, Kenni?" Betty had a habit of stringing her words together.

I cleared my throat and took a deep breath to gather my wits as I stared at Bosco Frederick lying with his legs half in the house and his torso half out of the house. His was staring toward the sky, his arms cast straight out to his side and a bullet hole right in between his eyes.

I took a step over him, being careful not to disturb anything.

"I'm going to need a backup squad at the Frederick home immediately." I clicked off and rolled the volume of my walkie-talkie down in case there was someone still there.

I flicked the snap of my holster, drawing out my gun. With my arms at full extension, I looked around, pointing the gun in every direction.

"Alma?" I called out her name when I noticed she was slumped over the table. "Alma? Sheriff's office. Come out if anyone is in here!" I screamed a couple of times in different directions.

The faint sound of sirens echoed through the open door.

"Sheriff's office!" I yelled again and stepped over to look at Alma.

My body stiffened. Her nails were painted Perfectly Posh. But I clearly remembered she wasn't wearing it earlier today.

I quickly did a sweep of the house and cleared it before Finn entered.

"Oh my God." His chest was heaving up and down. It was so hard for me not to lose myself into the warmth of his arms to let him assure me that everything was going to be okay. "Are you okay?"

"Yeah. I'm fine. Alma's nails are painted Perfectly Posh." I looked over his shoulder and stared at her. "Are they still wet?"

From where the light was shining in, the nails were still wet.

"She's not been dead long," I said.

"Bosco is still warm. I didn't feel a pulse, but I still called in an ambulance, just in case." Finn strapped his gun back in his utility belt and I followed suit.

Both of us worked like finely oiled machines until the EMTs got there. We secured the perimeter of the crime scene. We took photos and marked the gun that was next to Bosco's hand. It appeared to be a suicide. Only I wasn't sure how Alma got the polish or where the polish was. It appeared to be missing like it had been at Lucy's house.

"Kenni, you better get in here," Finn hollered for me as I bagged up the gun and the EMTs pronounced both Alma and Bosco dead.

"What?" I walked into the room they used as an office.

"Looks like a note was left on his computer." His gloved hand pointed to the computer screen in Bosco's office.

I leaned over to look at the screen.

"Lucy Ellen and I were having an affair. I'm not proud of

myself and have tried to stop it for several months now. Lucy Ellen was going to tell Darnell and even write one of those articles in the *Chronicle* like she always does. It would be too much for my Alma to take. In fear she'd leave me a lonely old man, I broke into Tiny Tina's salon."

I looked over my shoulder at Finn and sucked in a deep breath before I turned back round to continue reading.

"I knew exactly what nail polish Lucy Ellen loved because she'd complained about Tina refusing to do her nails. That night I left the camp in the woods and decided to poison the nail polish. I took it to her house that night because I knew Darnell was at the cabin and cleaning it. So I knew he wouldn't be home," my voice cracked as I read his sickening letter, "and I told her that I'd talked Tina into letting me buy the polish. She still said that she was going to reveal the affair even though I'd given her the polish as a peace offering, and that she was looking forward to typing the words to the *Chronicle* with her nails painted pink."

"This is awful." Finn shook his head from behind me and ran his hand down his face.

I swallowed hard and continued, "I left the cyanide at Tina's salon to plant the evidence. Then I went back to Lucy's and she'd already painted her nails and had died. I took the polish and put it in my hunting bag to get rid of when I went back to the cabin. This morning while I was in the shower, Alma came home from the Moose, cleaned out my hunting bag, and found the polish. She painted her nails with it since she'd been competing with Lucy Ellen on her spa days. When I got dressed I found Alma dead from the poisonous polish. That's how I've decided to take my own life. I just can't bear to live without the women I love."

"Where's the polish?" I asked and took the vibrating phone

out of my pocket. It was Tom Geary.

"Still haven't found it." Finn hit a few buttons on the keyboard to save the screen and turned the machine off. "I'll pack up the computer after I print off this note."

"I never saw this coming." I shook my head and put the phone up to my ear. "Hi, Tom. Do you have any information?"

"There are some disjointed prints on the cap of the cyanide bottle where the ridges of the cap had cut off some of the print. I can tell you that the prints on the fingernail polish aren't a match."

He confirmed that neither Tina's or Cheree's prints were on the bottle, making me think they really didn't have anything to do with Lucy's murder. "I put the jagged print in the database and there's nothing that's coming up."

This only made me wonder if Bosco was telling the truth. I'd never heard of Bosco getting in trouble with the law to see if we had fingerprints on file, but that'd be easy enough to find out.

"Did you send the report over?" I asked.

"I called you first, but I'll fax it right now. Anything else I can do for you?" he asked.

"Get Bosco's prints over to Tom." Poppa bounced on his toes. "If he truly did use the cyanide, then his prints would be on it. I arrested Bosco years ago for public intoxication and I fingerprinted him."

"I'm going to call over to dispatch and see if Betty Murphy can pull another set of prints and fax them to you." We clicked off the phone and instead of calling Betty on the walkie-talkie, I decided to call her.

"Kenni, what's going on over there?" Betty wanted firsthand knowledge.

"The Fredericks are dead. It looks like an apparent murder-suicide, but I'm not convinced." There was just a tug in my gut. "I need you to look up Bosco Frederick and get the fingerprints on file." I looked at Poppa, who nodded. "If I remember correctly, I do believe he was arrested years ago for public intoxication and he was printed. Can you send those prints to Tom Geary's lab?"

"I've got it covered." The phone line went dead.

"Kenni! Kenni!" A blood-curdling scream came from outside.

Finn and I took off running out of the cabin.

"Duke!" Tina yelled from the Jeep. She pointed to the side of the house. "He jumped out and is going nuts over there digging."

Duke was going to town with his nose stuck deep in the earth and his paws kicking up the wet dirt behind him.

"Duke!" I called. He looked up at me with a dumbfounded look on his face, his nose muddy, and his paws covered in it. "Drop it," I instructed him when I noticed something sticking out of his mouth.

Finn and I walked over to Duke, where he'd laid down with the item between his two front paws.

My mouth dried, my heart beat rapidly.

"The polish." Shock came out of Finn's mouth.

"The murder weapon." I sighed. "Duke, come." I patted my hand on my leg for him to come with me to the Jeep to get him away from the polish.

He darted back to the Wagoneer and took a leap back into the backseat.

"No!" I yelled, remembering the dress in the back and now his muddy paws were all over it.

"Don't worry. Maybe he'll make it prettier with the mud. It's so ugly it'd make a freight train take a dirt road." Tina's brow furrowed. "My polish. How on earth did it get here?"

"Bosco left a note saying he was having an affair with Lucy. Lucy Ellen was going to tell everyone about it and he couldn't let her do it." I gave her a quick recap of how he was the one who broke into the salon and how Alma got ahold of the polish.

Tina sat there in shock. Her eyes continued to take big long blinks.

"She going to be okay?" Finn asked.

"I think she might be in shock." I clicked on my walkie-talkie. "Betty," I called.

"Yes, Sheriff," she immediately answered.

"Can you call Max and tell him he needs to come to the Frederick home to pick up the bodies?"

"I'll call him." Her voice didn't hold the boisterous tone it had before.

While I was talking to Betty, Finn walked Tina back to the Wagoneer to sit down and gather her wits and called Wally Lamb to come pick her up. I secured the crime scene and took a lot more photos until I heard Wally pull up. Duke jumped out and lay next to the front tire.

"It was awful." Tina took Wally's cheap hanky out of the pocket of his polyester suit coat—I was sure it came from the local Walmart—and dabbed the corners of her eyes. "Like my daddy would say, I'm tougher than the backend of a shootin' gallery, but being behind bars about did me in."

"Now, now," Wally consoled her. "We'll get you home in no time."

Wally turned to me.

"Sheriff, we're just so happy that you finally brought the killer to justice. At least now that this case is over, my client can get back to her normal life, though a bit embarrassed, and the mayor will be happy because his bride will be happy." Wally

Lamb escorted Tina to his car.

Wally didn't waste much time giving me the look. He got in and zoomed down the Fredericks' driveway, nearly running Max Bogus's hearse off the road. Duke jogged next to his car, barking the entire time.

I stood there with Poppa by my side and watched as the hearse swerved and maneuvered back on the driveway.

"What are you still doing here?" I asked Poppa, who usually quickly disappeared as soon as a case was solved.

"I fear this isn't over." His words were bone-chilling. "I did my normal routine that I've always done after we solve a murder, but this time it didn't work. I walk into the fog and put the murder to rest, then I go around town scaring people away while keeping a close eye on you, but this time when I walked into the fog, it fell around my feet. It was the darnedest thing."

I tried to choke down a swallow to help bring some color back to my flushed face before Max got out of the car.

"Think about this." Poppa noodled an idea. "That letter from Bosco was written on a computer. Not handwritten and not saved. It was just too much explanation for me to even think it was from a distraught man. So he wrote the letter after he'd just found the love of his life dead, took the nail polish and buried it, all before he shot himself?"

"Why would he bury the nail polish?" I asked out loud.

"Good question. I was thinking the same thing." Finn startled me from behind. "Are you doing that whole talking to yourself thing again?"

"Yeah." I couldn't help but smile when I saw him. "I can't shake the notion that this isn't what it seems. It's all too perfectly packaged."

"And why bury the nail polish?" Finn asked my question.

Max Bogus got out of the hearse with a look of piss and

vinegar.

"Wally Lamb is crazy." Max shook his fist. "Did you see that he almost ran me off the road?" Max looked back toward the driveway, but Wally was long gone.

"I did," I said and turned to go back into the house.

"Murder-suicide?" Max asked.

The three of us took the steps and stopped shy of the door.

"That's what I thought when I first showed up. But I'm not so sure the facts will show that." I knew that Max had an obligation to do autopsies on both bodies since it was the law in Kentucky with a murder-suicide and since Bosco appeared to be Lucy's killer.

"I'm not saying Bosco didn't do it, but I agree with the sheriff. It wasn't as smooth as he made it seem in that letter," Finn told Max. He handed Max a piece of paper with the suicide note printed on it.

"I'm not sure what I'm going to find, but it appears that Bosco came in and found Alma dead from the polish he'd poisoned and killed himself." Max handed the letter back to Finn. "Only forensics will tell us the truth and that could take a few weeks."

We didn't have a few weeks. Cottonwood was already crazy with next weekend's wedding and this only added on the stress.

"Besides the whole cheating thing, which in itself is a huge motive to kill your spouse." Finn was right. Cheating was the third leading motive in murder cases.

"Duke." When I said his name out loud, I remembered how in the car on the way over he'd continued to try and smell Tina's fingers.

He jumped up and ran over to me. His tail was wagging so fast. I bent down to pet him. Finn took a treat from his pocket and fed it to Duke. Finn was so thoughtful when it came to

Duke.

"He was acting so odd on our way over here. He was trying to smell Tina's hands and fingers. I kept pushing him back because I thought he wanted to be scratched. I told him to stay in the Jeep when I got out, but he didn't. Next thing I know, he'd dug up the nail polish. Why did he want to smell Tina's fingers? How did he know to dig up the polish?"

"Maybe he picked up on the scent at the shop when you went to see Tina or he's been to Tiny Tina's with you and picked up on the scent there?" Finn questioned.

"You're probably right. He knew the smell and when his keen nose picked it up, he dug it up." I gave Duke a good rub along the head and neck. "Good boy. Good boy."

There were just some things Duke did that I couldn't explain and this was one of them.

"Yep, I got you one fine dog." Poppa proudly rocked back and forth on his heels.

"All I can do is let the autopsy speak for itself." Max headed on inside to take a look at what he had to deal with.

It was unusual to have to take two bodies at once to the morgue, but luckily his hearse could fit two church carts side by side.

While we let Max do his thing, Finn and I stood outside and pondered on what had just happened.

"This really doesn't make sense," I said to Finn. "I went to the gun show and talked to Alma."

"And?"

"Alma was there setting up for the show. I talked to her about Lucy Ellen and she believed Darnell was in jail for killing Lucy Ellen and she even acted as though they weren't friends. When I went back to the Lowells' I found photos of the couples on vacations and having dinners, and not just local." I pulled the photos out of my pocket. "I also went to see Darnell. He said that they'd always done things together, but Alma got jealous of Lucy. Or was it the other way around?" I thought for a second. "Maybe both were jealous of each other. Anyway, Darnell said that Lucy Ellen wanted to get Botox and all sorts of stuff done to compete with Alma."

"If you ask me, no amount of work was going to help Alma." Poppa was never one to shy away from the truth about anyone's appearance. "This morning she looked tired." He started flapping his hands. "I don't know much about women's nail polish, but I remember your mama flailing her hands around after she painted them when she was a kid. She claimed it took so long for them to dry." Poppa was good. He might not have realized he was onto something.

"And her nails." I smacked my hands together. "Alma's nails weren't painted this morning and she came home to paint them when it takes at least twenty minutes to be good and dry. But she was supposed to be at the gun show all day. She told me she would be. Plus Tina said that Alma didn't get the same nail polish because she didn't like Perfectly Posh. Alma only wanted the same treatments. So why would she paint her own nails Perfectly Posh when she didn't like the color?"

I opened and held the door for Max as he wheeled the first body out in a gray body bag.

"Maybe she found out about the affair and wanted to have her nails painted like Lucy Ellen when Bosco came home." Finn's eyes focused on the body bag. He grabbed the end and helped Max down the steps.

"Hmm. If the prints come back and Bosco isn't the killer, it looks like someone from the Hunt Club wants to silence anyone and everyone." Poppa sucked in a deep breath. As he exhaled, the air came out in long stream of fog. "Kenni, have you ever been to the huntin' cabins the Hunt Club uses?"

"No, but I think there's no better time to check it out," I muttered under my breath.

After Max cleared the bodies, it was time for Finn and me to get down to the nitty gritty and really look around.

"Are we still going out to the woods tonight?" Finn asked.

"Before I close this case by naming Bosco the murderer, I just want to check out the cabins and interview a few of the men that were there that night to see if Bosco said anything to anyone, or at least find out how he acted." It was going to be very interesting to see Finn in that environment.

"What time did you want to go?" he asked.

"Mama's big bridal supper is tonight." It reminded me that one week from tonight, I was going to have to give my first of two toasts. The first being the rehearsal dinner, the second was the wedding the very next day. "I'll make an appearance and then we'll go."

"Appearance?" He laughed and shook his head. "Your mama is really going to hate me."

"Nah." I winked.

One of the reserve officers took the computer back to the office so Betty could set it up. It was in those types of things Betty was worth her weight in gold. Since she loved to snoop and be nosy, combing through a computer was her thing. I think she really took pride in knowing the technology, which was sort of surprising since she was much older than the average techie. I wasn't techy, and since we kept it in house, if something did get out, I knew the source. Betty knew that too, which kept her from gossiping.

One thing I did know now was that I needed to stop by Camille Shively's office.

The waiting room was typical. The walls were painted gray,

and the carpet was gray with small white diamond shapes scattered about, and chairs lined the walls. There was a television hanging on the wall that played one of those twenty-four-hour news stations and a rack filled with all sorts of magazines was underneath that.

"Kenni, come on back." Camille stuck her head out the receptionist window and pointed to a door.

When I opened it, she was on the other side waiting for me. I followed her down a couple of halls until we made it to her office.

"What's up?" she asked. "Are you here about that whole happy fat thing? Because you don't have anything to worry about. Honestly. I had to talk your mom off the ledge about you dying from diabetes or heart disease."

"No. I'm here to ask you a few more questions about Lucy." I bit back anything snide I wanted to say about Mama. I knew her heart was in the right place, but once she got a topic in her head, she beat it like a dead horse.

"I told you everything the other day at Blanche's house." She walked around her desk and sat in the chair.

I remained standing and walked around as I talked.

"We have a confession." I looked at her fancy degrees framed on the wall.

"That's wonderful." Her voice rose. "Polly will be so relieved and happy that you can take the next week to really focus on her wedding and your big toast."

The big toast made me cringe.

"I need to tidy up a few loose ends." I turned around and noticed a picture of Camille all pretty on her graduation day. A big smile on her face. No wrinkles. Nothing. Perfect.

"Who killed Lucy?" There was concern in her voice.

"Bosco Frederick." I looked at Camille. Her brows formed a

V. "Apparently, Lucy Ellen and Alma were jealous of each other. Long story short, Lucy Ellen was on a mission to look younger. She'd been taking some pills. Darnell thought they were for her blood pressure. Do you happen to know what those pills were?"

Camille pushed her chair back from her desk and eased her head back and looked up at the ceiling.

"Oh my God. Why didn't I think of that?" she asked herself. "Kenni, remember you asked me about the blood pressure?"

"Yes." I took a seat in a chair.

"Well, she told me she was seeing stars and getting light-headed. I asked her if she'd been eating enough because she'd lost some weight. She assured me she was. There was no reason to not believe her. She'd always been a good patient. I got her initial blood test back. Nothing of huge concern, but I called to let her know we'd keep an eye on it. I don't think I got the long blood test results back yet." She clicked on her computer for a couple of minutes. "I think she might've been taking weight-loss pills." She picked up the phone. "Suzie, can you bring me Lucy Ellen Lowell's file please?"

"What did you find on your computer?"

"I logged into our system. Her blood results came back last night and I've yet to check my emails today. She tested positive for amphetamine. It's in diet pills." She eased back in her chair. "I told her not to take them. I wonder who she was getting them from."

"Darnell said she was thinking about Botox too." I took out my notebook and began writing down what Camille was telling me.

"What does all this have to do with her death?" Camille asked.

Her office door opened and Suzie, her nurse, walked over and handed Camille the file.

"I have to make complete reports and fill in all the holes." That was true, but Poppa was still lingering and I knew I had to figure out real fast who this killer really was.

"Here I made a note that she asked about wrinkle creams and Botox. We talked about the cost and she said something about Darnell not wanting her to spend money on those things because they were about to retire." She shut the file. "That was about all. But the diet pills she asked for are expensive, so if she was on them, which I believe she was, she was paying a pretty penny."

"Expensive." Poppa waltzed in out of thin air.

I looked at my watch. I still had time to make it to the bank. There was someone there I needed to see.

"Thanks for your time." I stood up. "I'll see you in a week at the wedding."

"I can't wait to see that dress on you." She scrunched up her pretty little nose.

"What are you thinking?" Poppa asked when we got back into the Jeep and headed to the bank.

"Hi, Kenni." Vernon Bishop came out of his fancy bank president office and greeted me. "What are you doing here?" He looked around like there was some trouble.

"Just here on a little business having to do with my investigation concerning Lucy Ellen Lowell." I nodded toward his office. "Can you talk in your office?"

He readily agreed. "I'm not sure how I can help, but I'll try."

He wore a nice three-piece pinstriped suit. His grey hair was neatly combed to the side. He wore the perfect amount of gel in his hair as well as cologne. He was much younger than he looked. He was about fifteen years older than me. His wife, Lynn, was a nice woman. She stayed home and cared for their three children who were scattered in ages.

They had a modest house in a typical neighborhood, but always looked well put together.

"Your mama has already got us working on the Christmas benefit." He smiled and offered me a seat and a sucker. I took both.

"I'm sure she does." I snapped the plastic wrapper off the sucker.

"I also heard you won't be here for the Christmas festivities." I nearly choked on the sucker. "I'm sorry. Did I misunderstand your mama?"

"You're right. I plan on going to visit Officer Vincent's family in Chicago, but I sure wish Mama would stop telling people." I bit the sucker off the stick. I was never able to really lick them down to the nub.

"We sure will miss your light-up Christmas sweater." He laughed.

If he only knew that Mama made me wear that darned thing every year to the Christmas tree lighting and the fights we'd have about it.

"Thank you. But I'm short on time." I tapped my watch. "Bosco Frederick has—"

"Died," he finished my sentence. "Small town."

"Yes. News does travel fast around here. Anyway, I wanted to see if you can tell me a little bit about Bosco's account."

"You know we freeze the account since we are a small bank and a small community." Vernon explained to me how most big banks didn't put holds on accounts, but since Cottonwood was a small town and somehow dishonest people trolled the obituaries, Cottonwood First National put holds on accounts until estates were settled.

"That's all fine and good, but I need to specifically know if there was any sort of payment made to Art Baskin or Danny

Shane."

He hesitated.

"You and I both know that I can get a warrant if necessary, but why don't we save the tax-payers money and just answer my question," I said, laying out the fact. Sometimes I found it was better to be upfront instead of beating around the bush.

"Bosco never came in, but I know about it because Darnell Lowell came in. He wanted to look at his 401(k). He mumbled something about not being able to retire and owing money to someone, but he was so antsy, I couldn't understand a word he mouthed." He clicked around on his computer. "He came in earlier asking about how much he had in his savings because of funeral costs for Lucy. He's sad. Very sad." Vernon's eyes grazed the top of his computer and he stared at me. "He seemed surprised when I told him that Lucy Ellen had cleared out that account a few weeks ago."

"She did?" I remembered the wad of cash she had in her hand at Tiny Tina's. "Did she say why she was withdrawing it?"

"She said that she was getting some work done." He shrugged.

"Like Botox? Diet pills? Did she mention any of that?"

"Diet pills?" He looked at me like every other man when I mentioned it. "I assumed she meant home remodel or something."

"No." I shook my head as I realized that poor Lucy Ellen was fighting so many inner demons.

"What does all this have to do with her death?" he asked.

"I'm not sure." I tapped the edge of his desk with my fingers. "Thank you for your time. I've got to run."

"See you at the big wedding!" he yelled after me. "I hear you're in it."

I nodded and waved. Mama. She sure didn't know how to

keep her mouth shut.

Even though I knew I should go home and get ready for not only Mama's shindig, but also the night at the cabin with Finn as we snooped around, but I had to go to the SPCA to see for myself that someone there wasn't bent out of shape over Lucy.

The sun was still out due to daylight savings time and the days were getting longer. It made me feel like I could get more accomplished in the day and since the sun was still up, so was the homestretch of this murder investigation. The trees were just starting to lose their full green leaves that were fed rich limestone soil through their trunks. The famous Kentucky bluegrass was starting to die along the old Military Pike Road that lead all the way out into the country where the shelter sat on fifteen acres of donated land.

The shelter did a lot of fundraisers and donation drives where they did really well. It didn't surprise me because the true heart of Cottonwood citizens showed when it came to the animals and in tough times in the community.

"Hi there," a young man greeted me when I stepped inside. He stood about five foot eight with a pageboy haircut, bangs dangled down into his eyes. "What can I do for you, Sheriff?"

He flung his head to the side, sending the bangs along with it and his brown eyes drew to my badge that was pinned on the brown shirt.

"I wanted to ask some questions about Lucy Ellen Lowell. A volunteer here." I made sure I continued to watch his face for any sort of discomfort while talking about her. Body language said a lot with words.

"We sure were sorry to hear about her death." His lips turned down. The frown reached his eyes. "She knew exactly how to get things we needed."

"What do you mean?" I asked.

"If the animals needed something and we didn't have it in the budget, she'd go out and get someone in the community to donate it or give a hefty dollar donation. She really helped us out." He let out a long sigh. "I'm afraid I'll never be able to find anyone like her that I can count on to get things done."

"That's nice to hear about her because I've heard some nasty things about her not getting along with people." I offered a slight smile. "Can you tell me if she had any problems with people here?"

"Not a one that I know of. She was always so giving of her time. She couldn't offer much financial assistance, but she did get people to donate. It was her way of being able to give back to the animals." As he finished talking, a girl walked through the door.

"Are you talking about Lucy?" She asked and tugged her blonde hair onto a ponytail using the rubber band around her wrist.

"I am." I took interest in what her take on Lucy Ellen would be. "Did you know Lucy?"

"Oh yeah. Everyone knew her. She was great. We all loved her. She did so much for the shelter that no one else has ever done."

"The shelter is about the only place in Cottonwood that she didn't write a review for." I pulled one of my business cards out of my front pocket. "If you remember anything or anyone that might've wanted to harm her in anyway, please don't hesitate to call. Anything." I wanted to make sure there wasn't anything that was too small to report.

Chapter Eighteen

"Do you think Lucy Ellen wanted to keep herself looking young because she really loved Bosco and wanted to leave Darnell for him?" Finn asked me.

I'd put on a one-piece denim jumpsuit with a pair of wedged sandals that Tibbie had dropped off from her Shabby Trends clothing line for me to wear to the big bridal dinner. While I stood in the bathroom in front of the mirror, Finn sat on the edge of the tub talking to me about the case.

"I don't know. I just know that Lucy Ellen had been spending all sorts of money when I know Darnell was planning on retiring." I brushed some lip gloss over my lips and rubbed them together.

"Do you think Darnell did it?" Finn asked.

"I've gone over and over the possibilities. I still want to talk to the other guys tonight about what they've seen or heard." I ran the brush through my hair one more time. "I can't explain it. It's like. . ."

He interrupted me, "I know. Woman's intuition. Remember, I've got a sister and a mother." He smiled and moseyed closer up behind me.

That's wasn't why. Poppa was why, but I couldn't tell him, so I let him just go with the intuition thing.

"Yep. I can't explain it." My eyes and jaw softened looking at him through the mirror. "It seems like an awfully complicated way to kill someone. To go through the motions of figuring out what Lucy Ellen wanted most that day, the nail polish, then researching that cyanide. It just seems like it's a crime that was very thought out."

"And Bosco couldn't do that?" he asked.

"I don't know." I gnawed on my bottom lip, scraping off some of the lip gloss.

"One thing I do know." He snuggled me, wrapping his arms around my waist. "You look beautiful."

"You don't think I have happy fat?" I asked.

He pulled away.

"Happy fat?" His face contorted. "What is that?"

"Nothing." I brushed it off. If I started to think about it now, I'd be mad at Mama all over again before I even made it to the dinner. "I've got to go make my appearance so we can go to the woods."

Duke left with Finn as I headed out to Mama's house. Duke and Cosmo would keep him company while he got ready the equipment we needed for our date night in the woods. Not that it really was a date night, but I thought it might be a little romantic under the big late summer moon. And the thought of a chilly night and needing a little snuggling wasn't such a bad thought either.

By the time I got to Mama's, I'd already dreamed up a romantic night instead of an investigation.

"You've got it bad, Kenni-bug." Poppa appeared just as I turned onto the street of my childhood home.

"I do. I can completely see myself with Finn Vincent for the rest of my life." I gulped. It was strange hearing myself say that when I really never took the time to figure out what I wanted out of life. "I've always been so happy being the sheriff here, having my girlfriends, my family, but somehow Finn makes it all complete."

"Being away for Christmas isn't weighing heavy on you? Because you love Christmas and you'd never miss the Christmas Festival."

"You're right. I do love it and I want to share that with Finn, but it's strange. It's like I've put my own needs and wants aside because I want Finn to be happy." My lips quivered as I tried to keep a big smile from emerging. "I can't believe that I'm actually happy to put someone else's needs before mine."

Not that I never did that before, but most times I put others before me because it was the good Southern girl thing to do.

"Oh no. You've really got it bad." Poppa's eyes teared up. "I bet you're gonna marry that boy one day."

"Why are you sad? You should be so happy that he loves me so much." I put the Wagoneer in park when I pulled up in front of my childhood red brick home.

"Because I'm not sure how you're going to feel about keeping me a secret. There should be no secrets in a marriage. Or a relationship that's heading that way." He brought up my worst fears about my relationship.

"I've thought about telling him, but every time I get ready to or think about it, something comes up and I just can't." I took notice of all the cars already at Mama's.

The days were getting shorter and the darkness was starting to blanket Cottonwood. Goosebumps pricked my skin. I wanted to blame it on the temperature dropping, but I knew it was from the thought of losing Finn when or if I told him about Poppa.

"I wonder if you told anyone about me how it would impact us." He looked at me. His eyes were hollow. "Would you still need me as your backup if he knew? Would I just go away?"

"I'm not willing to find out just yet." I closed my eyes to stop from crying at the thought and ruining my fresh face of makeup I'd taken the time to do for Mama's sake.

When I opened them, Poppa was gone. I took a second to collect my thoughts and get my emotions in check. I tugged the rearview mirror toward me and reapplied some lip gloss.

"I'm just going to meet his parents. It's not like he's asking me to marry him," I told my reflection, giving myself a good reason to keep my Poppa a secret a little longer.

"And to think she gave me a bad review before someone knocked her off" was the first thing I heard as soon as I walked through Mama's front door. "And to think they used my nail polish."

The warmth of comfort swirled around me as the familiar smells rushed over me. Home. There was nothing like it. I stood in the foyer and looked left into the fancy living room that was completely furnished from Goodlett's Furniture store, a locally owned business. The living room was rarely used. I took a couple of steps and entered the hallway. To the right were the three bedrooms, two on one side and one on the other, plus a bathroom at the end. To the left was the entrance to the family room and the kitchen along with an eating nook, laundry room, another full bathroom, and the door to the garage.

It wasn't a big house, but it was a comfy warm house my mama poured her heart and soul into because she loved to entertain. Many of those times, as a child, I escaped to my poppa's house.

The weather was so nice Mama had opened her windows and the door leading out to the back patio. The two nail stations were set up in the family room and the food and entertainment were on the patio.

"It was awful." Tina was hunched over her manicure table

doing a hand of one of Polly's bridesmaids who was from out of town. "Jail is not for gals like us."

I cleared my throat. Cheree jerked around from her manicure table and Mama, who was her client, looked up at me, as well as Tina and the gal in front of her.

"Kenni!" Mama wiggled her fingers toward me. "You're a bit late, but you're here."

"It's about time." Tibbie walked in with a glass of champagne with a cherry floating in it. "Polly has been freaking out."

"I had to work." I gave Tina a sideways smile.

"Oh, we heard." Mama drew back with an audible gasp. "Tina told us about Bosco Frederick killing Alma and Lucy. Just awful."

"And with my polish." Tina nodded.

"Shame, shame," Tibbie said, then took a sip. "Let's get you a drink."

"I'm not drinking tonight." I walked out to the patio with her and realized I didn't recognize any of the girls in Polly's wedding. "I've got to skip out early. Work calls."

"Nuh-uh. No way." Tibbie's eyes grew big. "You promised."

"I said I'd be here and here I am. I've got some things I need to check out with Lucy's case and it has to be tonight." Mama had done a fantastic job with the shower.

"Yay." Polly tapped her fingers together with a fake greeting when she saw me walk out the door. She grinned, winked, and gave me the finger wave from afar as she talked to someone on the other side of the patio. She had on a white dress that was fluffed way out with crinoline and a white wide-brimmed hat with a big silk bow tied under her chin.

There was a banner that read "Fiddle Dee Dee" strung over a snack table that held a tiny replica of Tara the mansion along with little figurines of Scarlett and Rhett. The cookies were in the shape of a woman's dress like Scarlett had and some cookies were decorated like hand fans. A little over the top, but adorable no less.

On The Run food truck was pulled up in Mama's backyard. Jolee had strung twinkly lights that hung over some café tables and chairs. Jolee was serving mason jars layered with BBQ beans, cole slaw and smoked BBQ chicken, shrimp and grits on toast, red velvet cupcakes with cream cheese icing, Southern pralines, mint julep cookies, cheese straws, watermelon, and peach tea punch. Everything I loved.

I reached for a piece of the shrimp and grits toast. Tibbie smacked my hand away.

"Ouch." I jerked away.

"The watermelon is for you." She jutted her finger out and gave me a grin.

"I swear. I hate all y'all." I rolled my eyes, knowing she was talking about that happy fat thing. "I'm not hungry."

"Fine." She turned around to look back at the party and I grabbed a mint julep cookie, stuffing it into mouth right as she turned back to me. "Kenni!"

"I am hungry," I muttered through the sweet treat as I chewed.

"Anyway, here is the game we are going to play. Do you think you can at least be here for that since you came up with it?" She handed me a piece of paper that I had clearly not come up with. "Polly or Scarlett" written in fancy script on the top. "Go with it. Polly thinks you came up with this game and she needs to feel loved by you."

"Really?" I asked with sarcasm. "Only for you will I go along with this."

There were a series of question with their names listed next to it and the guests had to circle which one was Polly and which one was Scarlett.

"Her favorite color is pink?" I asked, knowing Polly was wanting to get Perfectly Posh on her nails. "Really?"

"It's a game. Besides, you've solved the murder. And a week before the wedding. Polly and the mayor are so happy. Me too." There was excitement spewing from her. "I'm so happy you figured it out."

"Yeah. Me too." I swallowed the last of the cookie. The women's intuition Finn talked about earlier kicked in and I couldn't accept the fact that Bosco did it. It wasn't just the fact that Poppa was still here—it was the evidence that was just too perfect. "Excuse me."

"Where are you going?" There was a worried tone and look on her face.

"Inside." And then out the door, but I didn't say that.

I'd made my appearance. Polly had seen me and I'd get my nails done later.

"Okay. I'll see you in a minute." She handed me a piece of paper. "Here's your toast."

"You hold on to that for me." I headed on inside and bent down to Mama while she was getting the second coat of her nails painted. "Mama, I've got to go. Emergency."

"Kendrick," she scolded and jerked around.

"No, no, no, no." Tina wouldn't let go of Mama's hand. "You're going to smear."

"Kenni, no." Mama warned again. "You aren't doing this right now. You call Finn."

"Mama, my toast is written on a piece of paper that Tibbie has. You're so good at speaking in public." I waved bye and headed down the hall, getting myself safely out of the house only because Tina had a hold on Mama where she couldn't budge.

The temperature had dropped some more after the few minutes I'd been there. I even turned the heat on in the Jeep once I got in to take the chill out of the air.

"You ready?" I asked Finn when he answered his phone.

"That didn't take long."

"Mama was sitting in the nail chair and I figured it was a good time to skedaddle." It was all sorts of wrong and Mama was going to be really mad, but I had a job and it was an important one. "For some reason, I really feel that there's an urgency to us getting to the woods."

"Well, I'm ready. How far away are you?" he asked.

"I'm turning down Free Row now. I need to put on some jeans and grab a sweatshirt."

"Meet me in your driveway?" he asked. "I'll bring Duke back."

"Yep. We can take the Jeep." We said goodbye and hung up.

I hurried into the house and threw on my clothes, pulled my hair up into a ponytail, strapped my police utility belt around my waist under my sweatshirt, and grabbed my police bag from the table just in time to open the back door for Duke to run in.

I made sure he had some kibble and fresh water before I walked out the door where Finn was already in the front seat of the Wagoneer, Poppa right behind him in the backseat.

"If you hurry, you'll be able to talk to Danny and Art," Poppa said. "I went to the woods while you were stuffing your face with that cookie and they're all sitting around a fire discussing how they're going to come home since they've got to go to Lucy Ellen's layout at the funeral home tomorrow to pay their respects before Darnell moves out of town."

"Moving out of town?" I said.

"Who's moving out of town?" Finn asked with a funny look.

"Finn." I turned in my seat to him. "Do you think maybe Darnell Lowell killed Lucy?"

Chapter Nineteen

"Darnell?" He eased back into the seat. "I guess I never really suspected him."

"And that was his plan." I started to remember a bunch of little things about the investigation.

"Go on, Kenni, play the what-if game with him like you did me." Poppa encouraged me this time instead of discouraging me.

"You know I love my poppa a lot and I learned so much from hanging around the department from him." I gripped the wheel as we made our way out on Cottonwood Station Road, the curvy road that took us deep into the woods where the turn-off was for the hunting grounds the Hunt Club used. "Anyway, you and I can talk through clues using your whiteboard, but maybe now you and I can play the game that Poppa and I used to play."

"What's that?"

"The what-if game. With Darnell, I mean." There was a brief silence. "Like this. What if Darnell had an affair with Alma and Lucy Ellen found out, threatening to expose him because Lucy Ellen knew it would make Alma look bad to everyone, making her the ultimate winner in their little jealousy fight?"

Finn looked at me and teetered his head back and forth as if he were noodling the idea.

"What if Darnell killed Lucy Ellen using her favorite polish because she couldn't get it from Tina? He broke into Tiny Tina's. He somehow left the cabin unseen and then after Lucy Ellen was dead, he took the fingernail polish and hid it in the cabin.

"Bosco found it and put it in his hunting bag since he knew Alma would like it. Then Alma went home to question Bosco after I went to see her and she found the polish in his bag like the suicide note said, but the note was written by Darnell," I said, playing the what if game.

This was how Poppa and I used to work on his crimes when he was sheriff. It helped us think outside the box and maybe come up with some new leads to look into.

"Or Darnell was having an affair with Alma and he gave her the nail polish so she'd die too. He waited for Bosco to come home and he killed him, making it look like a murder-suicide, and wrote the confession about Lucy." Finn was good at this game.

"But why did he kill Lucy? Was she threatening to expose the affair? Was there an affair?" I threw out questions.

"There might be something in the timeline of that night and when Bosco was at the cabin compared to Darnell." Finn stared out the window.

"I guess we'll know here shortly." I turned the Jeep up the dirt road that took us back five miles until we got to the clearing where the Hunt Club members parked before they used their four-wheelers or hiked back.

"Kenni." He reached over and put his hand on my shoulder. "Thank you for sharing the game with me. I know your poppa stays on your mind a lot and I'm honored you opened up to me."

I choked back my emotions. This was not the time to be emotional. There was one thing I knew. I knew I loved Finn and I was going to have to start sharing all of my life, not just parts of it, with him if I truly did see myself with him for the rest of my life.

"We're here." I shoved the gearshift into park.

"Where are the cabins?" His head twisted around and looked at all the parked cars.

"Back that way." I pointed into complete darkness. "I hope you brought your flashlight."

We got out and unsnapped our flashlights from our utility belts. I gave Finn one of the reflective jackets I'd stuck back in the Jeep to put on so the guys wouldn't think we were some sort of game to shoot. I led the way. I'd been to the cabins many times in my life.

The night sky had fallen and it always seemed darker in the country. Even in the small town of Cottonwood, the little bit of light didn't make the darkness seem so black. In the country, you could see miles and miles of stars in the sky. If you stood still long enough and with a tiny bit of luck, you'd catch a shooting star.

We were silent most of the walk and about fifteen minutes later, there was an orange glow from afar.

"Sheriff here!" I yelled into the dark. "Danny Shane! Art Baskin!" I yelled out, knowing that I'd recognized their cars when I'd pulled up to park. "Sheriff Lowry here!"

"Sheriff?" The familiar voice of Art echoed into the night. "Is that you?"

"Yes! Deputy Vincent and I are here." I didn't have to yell as I got closer and closer.

There were six men around the fire when we walked up. Everyone greeted us, but there was a lingering curiosity in the air.

"We were just discussing going home tonight because we really need to support Darnell at Lucy's funeral tomorrow."

Danny said, followed up by echoes of agreement.

"Tomorrow?" I asked. I'd not heard anything about a funeral.

"He said with her body being part of the investigation, he was going to have a small memorial before he headed out of town," another one of the men said.

"Out of town?" I questioned.

"He said something about moving to his brother's down in..." he paused.

"Tulsa?" I asked.

"Yep." He snapped his fingers and pointed to me. "That's right. He said that he's decided to move to Tulsa for his retirement. I told him I'd pack up his stuff and bring it to him."

"What are you doing here, Sheriff?" Art Baskin asked.

"I'm here to actually talk to all y'all." I made eye contact with each of them. The fire flickered and sent an orange glow around the group. "I'm sorry for the loss of your president Bosco Frederick."

"Yeah, crazy stuff. I just can't believe he'd do something like that." One of the guys shuffled around. "Poor Darnell. He's not only lost his wife but also his best friend."

"Best friend?" At first I thought the guy meant Lucy, but I realized he was talking about Bosco. "I was under the assumption their friendship was over."

"Oh yeah. Bosco ended their friendship earlier in the summer. They'd been friends for over forty years. But Lucy Ellen started to get a little whacko over Alma and obsessed with all the success Bosco was having with the Jarrett company," Danny said before taking a swig of his bottle of beer.

"Jarrett as in the rifle company?" Finn asked.

"Yeah. He sent in a shot of a ten-point buck he caught last fall to the company using one of their rifles. They contacted him and did a big spread in their magazine," Art said and took the bottle of whiskey being passed around. He took a drink and passed it to Finn. "The article got picked up by many more hunting magazines and they did a big photoshoot with him and Alma. Bosco was so knowledgeable about hunting and guns they started paying him to write articles for them. It was good money too."

"Were Bosco and Lucy Ellen having an affair?" I asked.

"Hell no," a few of them men said collectively.

"What about Darnell and Alma?" I asked.

"Never. Darnell and Lucy Ellen were having financial problems, but nothing such as cheating." Art looked at Danny. "Lucy Ellen was caught taking money from the fund. We didn't press charges, and that's when Bosco had asked me and Danny to come down here and put in a few Lift cameras."

"Those cameras hunters put in the woods on trees and stuff. They're disguised and designed to work in any condition." Finn was surprising me for a city boy. "I saw something about that on the local public television station."

"They're pretty neat, but expensive." Art nodded.

"Do you have the footage for the camera?" I asked.

"Cameras. There's several. But yes, I have the technology to bring it up on my phone." Art pulled out his phone from this camouflaged jacket.

He used his finger, tapping his phone a few times before having everyone pass the phone down to me.

"Those are six cameras and you can click on the one you want to watch or watch all them at once," he said.

"Can we go back to the night Lucy Ellen was killed?" I asked.

"Yep. Just hit the three bars in the right corner and adjust the calendar to when you want. Technology is crazy nowadays."

He wasn't lying.

"Do you mind showing Finn all of Darnell's stuff you've bagged as well as the cabin he and Bosco shared?" I asked.

The next hour or so, I played with his phone and went back to the times Max had narrowed down Bosco's time of death. My eyes might've been tired, but I didn't see anyone leave the camp the entire time. Which made me believe that if Bosco didn't kill himself or his wife, whoever did this had nothing to do with the hunt club.

While I watched the camera footage, Finn got a lesson in hunting and a tour of the cabins. The only thing that bothered me was the fact that Darnell and Lucy Ellen had been having financial issues.

"Did you find anything?" I walked over to Finn.

"Nothing with Bosco." He took an envelope out of his back pocket. "I did find this in the cabin. It's a letter from the bank saying their account was overdrawn by one thousand dollars."

"Bosco's account?" I couldn't read it in the dark.

"No. It's addressed to Lucy Ellen and Darnell Lowell." He leaned in. "Do you think Darnell killed Lucy Ellen over money?"

Our eyes met. We stared at each other for a second before I decided it was time to wrap this up.

"Did any of you see Bosco or Darnell leave the night Lucy Ellen was murdered?" I asked and handed Art his phone back.

All of them shook their heads and a few of them yawned. It was getting late.

"Gentlemen." I walked around and gave each one a firm handshake. "Thank you for your information. Again, we are sorry for your loss."

"Can you send us a copy of the camera tape that the sheriff watched?" Finn was so good at collecting evidence.

"Sure will." Art nodded.

The flashlight showed us the way back along with a few lingering lightning bugs. In a couple of weeks, those cute fireflies would be long gone and not show up again until next summer.

"It's sad that Lucy, Bosco, and Alma will never see another firefly." My words disappeared into darkness and broke the silence on our walk back. My phone rang out and nearly scared me to death. "It's Max."

We stopped shy of the clearing where the cars were parked.

"What's going on, Max?" I noticed the time was well into the night.

"Some of the forensics came back, and I'm sorry to tell you that there's no way Bosco Frederick killed himself. From the path of the bullet, I can tell it wasn't from close range, nor was it from his gun." Max only confirmed what I was thinking.

"Thanks, Max. Can you send over what you've got so far?" I asked.

"What's up?" Finn asked on our way across the clearing to get back in the Wagoneer.

"He just confirmed that Bosco didn't pull the trigger. He was shot from afar." My mind went back through the crime scene.

The pictures in my head clicked between the kitchen table where Alma was found with wet nails and where Bosco was found lying halfway out the back door with the gun stuck in his hand. "Duke digging up the fingernail polish," I said.

"Are you doing that whole talking to yourself thing?" Finn questioned me as I started up the Jeep.

"Darnell and Alma were having an affair. She knew he killed Lucy, but she was still in competition with Lucy Ellen even after Lucy's death. He gave her the polish." My words trailed off. Then I looked up. "He killed Alma because she was going to come forward that he killed Lucy Ellen."

"And Bosco came home early from hunting, catching them off guard. Darnell keeps a gun on him with his conceal and carry. He pulled his gun and shot him, while Alma was sitting at the table dying," Finn suggested.

"On his way out, he buried the nail polish. Duke has been to the salon with me and he's been scratched on the head by Tina so much that he knew to find the familiar scent." I gulped and picked up my phone.

It was nearly midnight.

"I think Darnell killed Lucy Ellen because of money," Finn hit a nerve in my intuition, making me stiff.

"I went to the bank and Vernon told me Darnell had come in to check on his retirement account, but after Lucy Ellen died, he came in to get some money out of their savings to pay for a funeral for her. Vernon said Darnell was shocked to learn that Lucy Ellen had cleaned out that account a few weeks prior." I took a left off the dirt road and headed straight down Cottonwood Station Road.

Finn took out the envelope and opened it.

"This is dated a week ago." Finn continued to read. It had to be the account Vernon was talking about.

"I think our version of mine and my poppa's what-if game is turning into what happened." I looked at the big moon hanging overhead, hoping Darnell was looking at it because it was the last night that he'd be standing under it as a free man.

Chapter Twenty

The Wagoneer was the most uncomfortable place to try and sleep or at least rest my eyes. After the late night in the woods and after I'd dropped Finn off, I just couldn't sleep. I'd even stayed outside throwing Duke his ball into the fresh night air.

The thoughts about Darnell killing Lucy Ellen and the Fredericks made so much sense. The conversations I had with him over the past four or five days continued to haunt me. The things he'd say about how much he loved her and how was he going to survive without her made me think it was all a ploy for me to feel sorry for him. It scared me when I found out from the guys that he was going to skip town, so I decided I was going to do a stakeout.

Duke was my sidekick and we'd sat out in front of Darnell's house all night long. There was a U-Haul parked out front and a few lights on in the house. I'm not sure when he turned them off because I did doze off and got a crick in my neck.

Duke perked up and so did I when I saw his front door open.

"I dare you to get in that truck and take off," I warned him under my breath.

He walked straight past the truck and headed right to me. His eyes bore into the Jeep. I almost reached in the back to grab my rifle off the backseat because I was stupid enough to have left my utility belt at home.

"Sheriff." He handed me the cup of coffee in his hand. "Thought I'd bring you a cup of coffee. You deserve it after sitting here all night long."

"That obvious?" I shook my head in fear he'd poisoned the cup like he did the fingernail polish.

"I figured it was a matter of time before you thought I killed Lucy. Especially since there was tension between me and Bosco." He took a drink of the coffee, making me regret not taking it.

"So you don't mind if I call Deputy Vincent here to sit with you while I check a few things out?" I knew I wanted to go to the bank when they opened at nine this morning to check out his 401(k) and see if he'd cashed it in.

"Not at all." He held up the cup again. "You sure you don't want me to get you another cup while you wait?"

"No thank you." I was suspicious of how nice he was being.

As he walked away, I called Finn.

"Good morning." His voice made my heart skip a beat. "Want to come down for a cup of coffee?"

"I'm sorta not home." I knew he was going to be mad on a boyfriend level that I'd been on a stakeout, but happy that I'd thought of it on a professional level.

"You what?" His words were drawn out after I'd told him what I'd done and why I'd done it. "I'll be right there."

And he was. In no time I was on my way to the bank, only I knew they wouldn't let me in. Duke had his appointment with Bloomie at ten and I knew they opened up around seven thirty on Saturday. I'm sure Faith wouldn't mind if I dropped him off and then went to the bank.

Duke hopped out of the Jeep and ran straight up to Pet

Patch's door. When he heard the moo come from the bell, he howled. I heard Faith laugh from the back.

"Hey, Kenni." She waved to me with a pair of shears in her hand. "Back here in the grooming department. Come on back."

Duke darted around the shop looking for Bloomie and decided Faith was good enough for right now. With another good scratch, he headed back into the shop.

"I'm a little early," I said.

"That's fine. Duke's a good boy. He'll just hang out in here with me and Bobo." She pointed to the mini-poodle and walked over to the counter. She opened the cabinet. "Just the regular wash, flea bath, and dry?"

My eyes focused on the contents of the cabinet.

"Is that fingernail polish?" Poppa appeared next to Faith. "I swear that's the same fingernail polish that Tina Bowers makes."

"Kenni?" Faith called my name. "Are you okay?"

"I'm fine." I snapped out of the stare and watched as she opened the polish and started to paint Bobo's fingernails. "I didn't realize you painted dog nails."

I walked over to the framed license on the wall. There was one for her and one for Bloomie. The dates caught my attention.

"Didn't you say that your license was expiring soon and you just went to the pet expo to renew it?" I recalled what she'd told me when I asked her about Lucy. "It looks like Bloomie's was just renewed and you did yours a couple months ago."

When I heard the glass of the nail polish knock against the steel counter Bobo was standing on, I turned around.

"I think I'd like to see those airline tickets with your name on it." I watched her reaction with a keen eye.

"I...um..." She hem-hawed around for a second and then opened a drawer up. "It's in here somewhere." She shuffled papers and reshuffled them. When she looked up at me, her face was as white as I thought a ghost's face would be. But not Poppa's.

I knew right then and there that she was the killer. I felt for my holster and realized for the second time this morning that I'd left my holster at home. "Why did you kill her? Why did you kill Alma and Bosco?"

I kept my eyes on her hand as she slid it across the table and grabbed the shears, the very pointy shears.

She brought her hands to her sides.

"Do you know how hard it is to make a go of a business in a small town? When someone like Lucy Ellen Lowell decides to get mad, she takes out her anger on me and my business. I had to listen to whispers and deal with people staring at me. People who bought animal products from me started going to Dixon's Foodtown to purchase items." Nervously, she took the shears and dragged them back and forth at her thigh, cutting her khaki pants and drawing blood. "The last time I'd gone to Tiny Tina's, Alma Frederick was in there. She apologized to me for Lucy's behavior and she told me how they'd stopped being friends. When I went to the Chamber of Commerce meeting last month, I overheard Vernon say that Lucy Ellen Lowell was spending money like crazy."

She lifted the scissors up to Bobo. My immediate reaction was to pummel her to the ground, but without my own weapon I stayed still.

"Don't hurt Bobo." My voice was stern.

"Idiot. I'm grooming him." She cut a big chunk of fur and it floated to the counter. She cut another chunk.

"Why did you kill them?" I asked in a very calm voice.

"When you came around here the other day questioning my whereabouts, I knew you weren't on the trail of Darnell. I'd planned it so well. But you were so stupid. I can't believe I voted for you." She snarled. "I knew I had to kill Alma too. With all the rumors going around, I knew if I killed her it would appear that the rumors about Darnell and her were true. It was her husband that I didn't expect to come home." She took a step back from the grooming table and pointed the sheers at me. "I don't even know if Tina remembers telling me how to make polish because it's been so long ago. Years in fact. When I told her I was painting my clients nails, she gave me her little tip on making nail polish. It was perfect for me and easy to break into her shop and make the nail polish. After I put just enough cyanide in my Perfectly Posh, conveniently I left the bottle in Tiny Tina's. There's so much junk back there, I knew she wouldn't notice an extra bottle, much less the cyanide bottle." There was a very satisfied smile growing across her face.

I heard Duke's nails clicking on the tile floor of the shop getting closer and closer.

"Ah, Duke." Her eyes lowered as she looked towards the sound of the clicking. "I never figured he'd find the polish I'd buried at the Fredericks. He's a hell of a lot smarter than you."

"Here boy." Poppa came in ahead of him and called for him. Duke was the only one other than me that could see my Poppa. "Get it!"

"Glad I got this little guy." She bent down and lifted up the hem of her pant leg, exposing a small handgun. She unclipped it out of the ankle strap and when she stood up, she put the gun on the counter with her hand positioned perfectly for firing.

Duke walked in. His nose went straight up in the air and I could tell his eyes focused on that nail polish next to Bobo. My instinct kicked in and so did Duke's. Both of us lunged at the same time. He went for the nail polish and I went for gun.

Faith scattered after it too, but I grabbed it before she got it, and Duke grabbed the polish. Poor Bobo was yipping and yelping, shaking in fear.

"Hold it right there!" I yelled and pointed Faith's gun at her. "Don't you move a muscle because I have no problem putting a bullet in your leg, arm, or chest."

Duke looked between Faith and me. He dropped the bottle and stiffened, giving Faith a low growl.

"Good boy. Good boy." Poppa danced around behind Faith.

Little did she realize that Duke was growling at Poppa to play with him even though he looked like he was going to attack her.

"I'm not going anywhere." Faith dropped her head and began to sob.

One week later... Wedding Day

The week leading up to Polly's wedding was one filled with forgiveness and fluff. The forgiveness was between Tina Bowers and me. By all rights, she'd been a fraud for many years under the fake certificate that said she was a massage therapist. Like I told her I would, I went before the judge with her charges. Luckily, she was only given a hefty fine and had to prove that she was now a legal therapist. Unfortunately, the judge also took away the shop's certification to do massages for one year, but she could still do manicures and pedicures. On the upside, she wasn't going to the state pen.

Then there was Darnell. He was sad and lonely. He'd not only filled Lucy's big shoes at the SPCA, he ended up adopting a dog that seemed to keep him busy. He named her Lucy. He even stepped in to fill the open president's position at the Hunt Club. He was going to be okay after all.

We'd all gone to Faith's sentencing, where it was decided she'd spend the rest of her life in the state penitentiary for the murders of Lucy Ellen Lowell, Alma Frederick, and Bosco Frederick. She said at the sentencing that she'd done all of Cottonwood a favor by getting rid of Lucy Ellen and that we should thank her. I thanked the judge for locking her up.

Another person I had to make amends with was Mama.

She'd worked so hard to have such a nice bridal supper for Polly the night I'd skipped out. This week nothing made Mama more happy than going with me to my final fitting at Blanche's, a girl's day at Tiny Tina's getting the manicure I'd missed the night of her house, and fixing supper for me and Finn a couple of nights that included things that didn't feed my happy fat.

Finally, I made amends with Polly Parker. With the murders solved, I made sure that I was at her disposal all week long. I took every single phone call from Tibbie and every text message from Polly.

Even the frantic one the afternoon of the wedding.

"You've got to get over here right now." Polly was crying on the other end of the line.

"On my way." I groaned and got up from the couch.

It was so hot today, the squirrels were putting suntan lotion on their nuts, as my poppa would say if he were here. He'd not been around all week, which told me he still was only my guardian ghost during an active murder investigation.

"Duke, you've got to stay here all night."

His head twisted left and right like he understood before he laid back down. It was even too hot for him to go out and run for his ball.

"I'll leave extra kibble and water," I called behind me when I walked down the hall to get the maid of honor's dress and bonnet. Everyone was going to the wedding or I'd have gotten Mrs. Brown, my neighbor, to watch him. Or Jolee, or Finn, or even Mama. I was a little thankful for the bonnet. My honey brown hair was stick straight, but something about high humidity really put a crazy wave in it. And it wasn't pretty like those beach waves those crazy tools did to the girl's hair in those infomercials.

With my outfit for the wedding in my hand, I grabbed the

little cosmetic bag filled with what little makeup I used, headed out the door, and a few minutes later pulled up to the back parking lot at the Cottonwood First Baptist Church.

"Thank God you're here." Tibbie Bell was sprawled out on a folding chair with her legs straight out in front of her and one of the wedding favor fans in her hand, vigorously waving it over her face. "I can't take another minute in this hot weather."

"This should go into your party-planning book." I couldn't help but notice she was glistening with sweat.

"What would that be, Kenni?" she asked with a sarcastic tone.

"Keep in mind the crazy weather in between seasons in Cottonwood." I couldn't help but smile knowing Polly had driven her over the edge. "I think a few years ago it was snowing on this exact same date."

"Kenni, this is no time to talk about the past. It's the here and now, and right now I think I want to string up our bride by her bra straps." She fanned quicker.

"Oh no. What does she want you to do now? Sue Mother Nature?" I joked.

"Not funny." She pointed the fan to the church. "Go on. Go in there and take a look."

I shrugged and headed inside with the hanger flung over my shoulder. It was going to be a little uncomfortable with that big dress on in this heat, but I was bound and determined not to complain and keep the peace between me and Polly, at least until tomorrow.

"Kenni." Polly's shrill voice stabbed my ears. "Look at this." She pointed to what I assumed was her cake. "The air conditioning is broken and the cake is melting. Look at the bride." She pointed to the sugary figure on top that was distorted. "That's supposed to be me."

She broke out in tears.

I reached out with a reluctant pat on her back.

"Look at my hair." Her words seethed with anger. "It's falling out. All the Scarlett curls are falling out and Tina Bowers has no idea how to fix it. And this makeup." There was a visible line that ran along her jaw. "It's melting off my face. I hate the weather here!"

She stomped toward the door that led out to where Tibbie was still fanning herself and smacked them open.

"Tibbie Bell! You're fired!" Polly screamed and headed back inside, disappearing into a room. She slammed the door.

Tibbie held up her hand and gave Polly a not-so-nice gesture and continued to fan herself.

There was only one person that could handle this, and it wasn't me.

Toots Buford didn't waste any time driving to the church from the time I called her. When I saw her 1965 pink VW bug pull into the church parking lot, the stress melted off of me.

"Where is she?" Toots hurried in with all sorts of bags hooked on her arms.

"She's right in there. Toots." I stopped her before she hurried in to rescue her best friend. I draped the maid of honor dress over her shoulder. "I think this is for you. Consider it my wedding gift to Polly."

Toots's bright red lips, that matched her bright red hair, drew up into a huge smile. She sent an air kiss my way before she disappeared into the dressing room to put her magical touch on her best friend.

"Move over," I instructed Mama once the organist started to play the song the bridesmaids were walking down the aisle to.

She looked at me with a horrified look on her face.

"Don't worry," I whispered and made her scooch some

more to make room for Finn. "Polly exchanged me for Toots. It's all good."

Mama wasn't about to throw a hissy fit right there in front of everyone. She and Daddy scooted down, making enough room for me and Finn.

I had to admit the wedding was beautiful, especially now that I didn't have to wear the green hoop dress. Preacher Bing had used the church's emergency fund to call a heating and air conditioning contractor from Clay's Ferry to fix the HVAC unit. Needless to say, there was nothing wrong with it. The weather had been so chilly last week, Preacher Bing had forgotten he'd turned off the air conditioning and when the HVAC mechanic flipped it back on, Preacher Bing simply said a prayer and asked me to keep it between us. The rest of the wedding went off without a hitch.

The reception was everything Polly Parker Ryland wanted. It was *Gone with the Wind* on steroids. The entire inside of the reception hall looked like the movie set of Polly's favorite movie, down to the green velvet curtains.

"I still can't believe you are taking my baby to Chicago for Christmas." Mama cried in her cocktail at the reception.

"Ignore her," I instructed Finn. "Don't look at her."

"Kenni, why do you have to be so disrespectful?" she asked.

"Ladies, all the single ladies," the smarmy voice of the DJ called out. "It's that special time of throwing the bouquet."

"Get up there right now." Mama pointed to the front where Polly was twirling her bouquet around her head. "You're already breaking my heart about Christmas. Just act like you want me to be happy."

"Fine." I rolled my eyes and pushed back my chair.

As soon as I stood up, it was just like the other wedding when I planned in my head how I'd keep my hands to my side and not participate. The bouquet went flying in the air. The single ladies in front of Polly stopped jumping when they realized the flowers had passed over their head and they turned around, watching as it went into a free fall, hitting me smack dab in the forehead and falling on the floor next to my feet.

"Your parents are going to love my Kendrick." Mama's voice oozed with happiness.

TONYA KAPPES

Tonya has written over twenty novels and four novellas, all of which have graced numerous bestseller lists including *USA Today*. Best known for stories charged with emotion and humor, and filled with flawed characters, her novels have garnered reader praise and glowing critical reviews. She lives with her husband, three teenage boys, two very spoiled schnauzers and one ex-stray cat in Kentucky.

Henery Press Mystery Books

And finally, before you go...
Here are a few other mysteries
you might enjoy:

PILLOW STALK

Diane Vallere

A Madison Night Mystery (#1)

Interior Decorator Madison Night might look like a throwback to the sixties, but as business owner and landlord, she proves that independent women can have it all. But when a killer targets women dressed in her signature style—estate sale vintage to play up her resemblance to fave actress Doris Day—what makes her unique might make her dead.

The local detective connects the new crime to a twenty-year old cold case, and Madison's long-trusted contractor emerges as the leading suspect. As the body count piles up, Madison uncovers a Soviet spy, a campaign to destroy all Doris Day movies, and six minutes of film that will change her life forever.

Available at booksellers nationwide and online

Visit www.henerypress.com for details

FIT TO BE DEAD

Nancy G. West

An Aggie Mundeen Mystery (#1)

Aggie Mundeen, single and pushing forty, fears nothing but middle age. When she moves from Chicago to San Antonio, she decides she better shape up before anybody discovers she writes the column, "Stay Young with Aggie." She takes Aspects of Aging at University of the Holy Trinity and plunges into exercise at Fit and Firm.

Rusty at flirting and mechanically inept, she irritates a slew of male exercisers, then stumbles into murder. She'd like to impress the attractive detective with her sleuthing skills. But when the killer comes after her, the health club evacuates semi-clad patrons, and the detective has to stall his investigation to save Aggie's derriere.

Available at booksellers nationwide and online

Visit www.henerypress.com for details

DOUBLE WHAMMY

Gretchen Archer

A Davis Way Crime Caper (#1)

Davis Way thinks she's hit the jackpot when she lands a job as the fifth wheel on an elite security team at the fabulous Bellissimo Resort and Casino in Biloxi, Mississippi. But once there, she runs straight into her ex-ex husband, a rigged slot machine, her evil twin, and a trail of dead bodies. Davis learns the truth and it does not set her free—in fact, it lands her in the pokey.

Buried under a mistaken identity, unable to seek help from her family, her hot streak runs cold until her landlord Bradley Cole steps in. Make that her landlord, lawyer, and love interest. With his help, Davis must win this high stakes game before her luck runs out.

Available at booksellers nationwide and online

Visit www.henerypress.com for details

GHOSTWRITER ANONYMOUS
Noreen Wald

A Jake O'Hara Mystery (#1)

With her books sporting other people's names, ghostwriter Jake O'Hara works behind the scenes. But she never expected a séance at a New York apartment to be part of her job. Jake had signed on as a ghostwriter, secretly writing for a grande dame of mystery fiction whose talent died before she did. The author's East Side residence was impressive. But her entourage—from a Mrs. Danvers-like housekeeper to a lurking hypnotherapist—was creepy.

Still, it was all in a day's work, until a killer started going after ghostwriters, and Jake suspected she was chillingly close to the culprit. Attending a séance and asking the dead for spiritual help was one option. Some brilliant sleuthing was another-before Jake's next deadline turns out to be her own funeral.

Available at booksellers nationwide and online

Visit www.henerypress.com for details

Made in the USA
Coppell, TX
09 August 2021

60234979R00134